The Iron Dragonfly

Troy Dust

The Iron Dragonfly
A Novel

FSC
www.fsc.org
MIX
Papier aus ver-
antwortungsvollen
Quellen
Paper from
responsible sources
FSC® C105338

Originally published as

Die Eiserne Libelle
Copyright © 2012 by Troy Dust

by Zeilenwert GmbH, Rudolstadt, Germany
(2013, eBook, no longer available)

Republished in 2019 as eBook
by BoD – Books on Demand, Norderstedt, Germany

Original English translation by Rebekka Pattison and Emily Pattison. Final editing by Troy Dust with additional help + support by Noël Kugler.

The Iron Dragonfly
Copyright © 2021 by Troy Dust

Cover + Design by Troy Dust

Printed and published by:
BoD – Books on Demand, Norderstedt, Germany

ISBN: 978-3-7534-2445-3

»This is a truth: when you sacrifice your life, you must make fullest use of your weaponry. It is false not to do so, and to die with a weapon yet undrawn.«

Miyamoto Musashi
›The Book of Five Rings‹

Sundown

He could hear indistinct voices, and the faint sizzle of a fire nearby.

His body was heavy. It felt like he was sinking, sinking further and further downwards. As if any second the ground would open up and swallow him whole. Practically every muscle in his body was aching, forcing him to keep still.

A fresh breeze caressed his face, bearing the scent of flowers and the sea.

Slowly, he opened his eyes. The fading daylight revealed a magnificent vaulted ceiling at least 30 metres above him. But before he could focus on somewhere in the upper left-hand corner of his field of vision, where he could almost imagine a hidden piece of sky, his heavy eyelids closed and obscured the world from view once more. And before the silence could descend upon him again, he heard someone begin to strum quietly on a guitar ...

Chapter 1

The Visit

Gwinard stepped into his light-flooded bedroom.

A gigantic screen took up the entire right-hand wall showing an expansive grassland swaying in the wind, huge clouds swept across the meadow, starkly contrasting white and grey against the blue sky.

This display, together with the square bed directly in front of the screen, was reflected in the glazed wardrobe that took up the whole of the left-hand wall. Across from the door was a window that stretched across the complete width and height of the room. It wasn't possible to open the window – in fact, all the windows in the flat were just plain glass panels. Fresh air was pumped into the rooms by the air conditioning. He had been lucky with where his flat was located within the building – nothing was better than daylight. He had lived in enough dumps without windows in the past, some hadn't even had air conditioning.

Holding a dirty t-shirt and worn socks in his hand, he headed towards the laundry basket in front of the wardrobe next to the window. He was only wearing shorts. Raindrops from the last shower meandered across the glass, blown to the left by the wind. Beyond the window, Gwinard could make out huge buildings made of steel, concrete and light natural stone. The buildings were mostly laid out in a combination of symmetrical circles, ellipses and ovals. The actual streets lay hidden in the mist with the buildings rising like pillars from a dense fog that drudgingly drags itself across the ground. In the part of the city spread out before him, most buildings were shorter and well below where Gwinard was standing, so he was able to make out the line of the sea and the horizon beyond the city. Columns of clouds seemed to be bearing the weight of the sky above the buildings.

Upon this scene, the sun had painted a double rainbow, mirrored by yet another rainbow to the left of it. This colourful trio reached up into the heavens. On the rooftops below him, he could see meadows, trees and even copses, as well as patches of green on ledges and in niches, which loosened up the architecture of the enormously bulky buildings.

The building, in which Gwinard had been living for the past five years, was home to more than 230,000 people spread over 257 floors – and this wasn't even the largest building in the city. For 7 years, he had been working for the waste collection service. It wasn't the best sort of job one can have, but it certainly wasn't the worst – and the pay was good. Besides, he could have ended up as a worker down the sewers, or in a factory on a conveyor belt, as a gatherer on one of the gigantic landfill sites or poor and homeless on the street. Now he was 28 and he had no idea how long it would continue like this and where else he might wind up.

Gwinard threw his dirty clothes into the laundry basket, turned around and left the room to wash off the sweat, the dirt and especially the stink of the day in the bathroom just opposite this room. In the shower, the water ran down his toned body and his fair hair stuck to the contours of his head, while steam condensed on the window and the mirror above the sink. He turned off the water and reached for the shower gel. The cap opened with a click. He was just about to squeeze some gel onto the palm of his hand, when he heard noises above the sound of water dripping from the calcified showerhead. Since these gigantic, anonymous complexes were often targeted by burglars – at all times of the day and night – he placed the shower gel on the shelf and left the small shower cubicle as quietly as possible. A surge of adrenalin sharpened his senses and he crept to the door and listened: someone was clearly just disappearing into a room, because the footsteps were growing quieter.

Gwinard looked around; he knew that the door was his only way out, so he searched for an object to use as a weapon. Lying on the sink, he saw his nail scissors. He reached for them, took them in his right hand and formed a fist, with the sharp tip of the scissors protruding from between his forefinger and middle finger. Still wet from the shower, he hastily slipped back into his shorts – right now he didn't mind that he hadn't taken any fresh ones into the bathroom. He listened at the door and heard someone ransacking one of the rooms. By the sound of it, the person was searching for valuables, and was in a hurry.

The kitchen was located to the left of the bathroom and opposite that – next to the bedroom – was the living room. To the right of the bathroom there was a storage room, and opposite that a room where he kept his paperwork and his collection of books in various shelves, drawers and cupboards – which is why he called it "the office," even though it wasn't one really. At the right end of the hallway was the main door to the flat. Next to it was a small coat stand with an integrated mirror.

It wasn't possible to make out how many intruders were in the flat, or where each of them was at that moment. He only knew that he had to make it out of this trap, into the hallway and out of the flat. Here he was a dead man. Getting out fast was his only chance, regardless of whether the intruders had weapons or not.

Gwinard looked down at the door and hoped that no one was standing directly on the other side, waiting for him. In his mind's eye, he went through the individual steps.

He calmly breathed in and out. Then he tensed his muscles and ripped the door open. He stormed to the right and noticed two things: the door to the flat was ajar and the noises came from behind him, so either from the living room or from the kitchen.

Suddenly a man was standing in the doorway to the storage room. Before he could react, Gwinard took aim at his head and punched him hard with the nail scissors still in his fist. He struck the surprised man's cheek, and felt how the scissors got caught in the flesh. The sudden blow and the combination of wet feet and smooth, synthetic floor, made him briefly lose his balance and stumble. With his left hand, he tore the door open. He stormed out and to the right – to the left there was merely a wall with a fire extinguisher and a glass fire alarm box.

Gwinard ran across the cold concrete floor without even glancing over his shoulder. The swerving corridors with their dirty lamps, fire detectors and sprinkler heads in the middle of the ceiling all rushing behind him. After about 50 metres, he reached the lifts for his section. There were 10 lifts on each side of the corridor. On the left, the doors to the third lift stood open. He rushed in and typed the digits "1-0-5" into the worn out key panel – the floor where a colleague and friend lived.

Once both wings of the door had slid closed, out of breath, he looked at his right hand. The blood on the scissors and on his knuckles already begun to dry. He could feel the heel of his hand pulsating with pain.

After what felt like an eternity – although it was just a few seconds – the lift slowed down and stopped after dropping 83 floors. The doors opened. Gwinard ran to the right and then into one of the side corridors on the left to reach his destination, where he urgently needed to borrow clothes and consider his next steps.

Chapter 2

Chaos

Half an hour later the two men stood – each smoking a cigarette – in front of the empty shelves and stripped cupboards in Gwinard's office. All the books and files lay strewn across the floor, even the drawers of the cupboards had been ripped out, emptied and thrown to the ground. Similar scenes of chaos could be found in the rest of the flat. Byrd had given Gwinard some clothes and listened to him carefully while the latter got dressed and described what had happened. They had then gone back to Gwinard's flat, each armed with a baseball bat and a carpet knife, only to find it abandoned and ransacked.

"Did you have any money here?" Byrd asked, while looking for an ashtray. Gwinard left the room without replying, returning shortly thereafter with an empty jam jar that he had filled with a little water.

"It's still here," he replied and held out the jar to Byrd.

"Is anything else missing?"

"To be completely sure of that, I will have to tidy up. But as they didn't even take the money from the kitchen, I'd be very surprised. The can I always keep it in was lying on the table, the money right next to it. I've just pocketed it now."

Byrd lightly tapped his cigarette against the edge of the jar to loosen the ash. "Then they were looking for something else. But what? Or they went to the wrong apartment. That can happen quite easily here."

Gwinard took a deep drag on his cigarette. He was groping in the dark. Why would someone break into his place and not even take the chance to steal his money?

Byrd gave him a sceptical side-long glance. "Or have you been getting up to anything recently? Fought with anyone?"

Gwinard began to think in earnest. He didn't have any enemies – as far as he knew – and he wasn't having any trouble with the dealer he occasionally bought first-class weed from. It didn't make any sense at all that someone would break into his flat without taking anything.

"Or have you seen something you shouldn't have? Perhaps someone wants to scare you."

"Not consciously," Gwinard replied, taking a last puff on his cigarette and dropping the stub into the jar before passing it to Byrd.

"Sometimes we unintentionally see things we shouldn't in our jobs, as you know." He stepped over the books and files to get to the window and let his gaze sweep over the city. The sky had darkened a while ago and now it was pouring with rain.

Byrd also let his half-smoked cigarette fall into the glass which he then placed on one of the cupboards. "What are you going to do now?"

Gwinard turned around. "I'm going to clean up and install a new lock." He looked around, taking in the chaos and reckoned that he would need quite some time to get his flat back to the state it had been in a few hours ago.

"No police?"

"What for? The most valuable thing here was the money and they didn't take it. And you can't make any money out of any of the books either."

Byrd shrugged his shoulders. "I think I still have a spare lock at my place. You should definitely put that in before you go and buy a new one."

"That would be useful."

"I'll go and get it," said Byrd. He left the room to make his way back to his flat. In the corridor, he picked up one of the baseball bats that they had left leaning against the wall and took it with him.

Gwinard paused for a second to take in the mayhem. It was as if a wave had swept through his flat, as if some sort of liquid had covered the floor that would now evaporate bit by bit. He gave an irritated sigh, pulled himself together and crouched down to start picking up the books to put them back where they came from.

Chapter 3

A Hunch

While Gwinard made use of the weekend after the incident to clear up the chaos, he mulled over some of the possible reasons for someone to break into his flat.

In doing so, he stumbled across an idea that made him stop in his tracks. He was sitting on the floor cross-legged, trying to sort out the mountains of paperwork and put things back where they belonged.

What if this hadn't been a coincidence or a mix-up? Someone could have been spying on him and finally struck that day, without knowing that he would be at home. This seemed plausible because they had immediately started to turn the apartment upside down, instead of first searching and securing all the rooms – including the bathroom; or maybe amateurs had been at work that didn't know any better. But what if they didn't care whether he was in the flat or not?

The thought that had interrupted his task was the memory of something that had happened a couple of weeks ago:

On the waste truck's last tour through a run-down neighbourhood before he got off work, he had spotted a large cardboard poster tube that someone had covered with a grey rubbish bag. Because the bottom end had been placed in a see-through plastic carrier bag, it was possible to see what it was. He had noticed it several times over the last few days, leaning against the corner of a house, not far from the waste containers he had to empty. It was placed behind an old fridge that had been there for so long Gwinard couldn't even remember how long it had been standing there; it was just part of the scenery.

The following day he and his colleagues were assigned a different route for a week, before being sent back on their usual route – the one with the mysterious tube and its hidden secrets.

In the shadow of an aerial cable car passing overhead, Gwinard pushed the last waste container back into its usual place in the backyard. As he turned around to go back, his gaze fell between the wall of the house and the fridge, where the strange cardboard tube was still standing. Without even wondering if and why someone might have forgotten the tube – probably just like someone had forgotten the fridge – and without thinking about what could be inside, he walked up to it, bent over some bricks, glass bottles and tiles that littered the ground, and picked up this object that seemed so out of place. He pulled off the rubbish bag and the plastic carrier bag and threw them both into the recently emptied container.

The unlabelled tube was slightly longer than a metre and was approximately 20 centimetres in diameter. It weighed around six to eight kilograms. The white plastic lids on both ends were secured with layer after layer of brown packing tape.

Gwinard placed the tube over his shoulder and left the backyard. He turned right, where the waste collection truck was already standing in front of the entrance to the next backyard. He opened the passenger door and threw his discovery into the driver's cab.

"What's that?" asked the driver and looked over the newspaper he had laid out across the steering wheel.

"Just some wallpaper patterns," Gwinard lied clumsily. He wanted to add something, but the driver was already back to reading an article, so he just turned around, shut the door and went back to work.

Once he had finished work, Gwinard placed the tube in his locker and got changed. Because he was in a bit of a hurry, he decided to take it home the next day ...

He couldn't believe that he had forgotten it; simply because he had leant the tube against the back of his locker and unintentionally hidden it behind the clothes hanging there.

Out of sight, out of mind.

Could this tube really be the reason why his flat had been broken into?

This idea was reinforced by the fact that the perpetrators had seemed to have a certain routine and calmness to them, because they had searched through everything, even after he had run outside, and they hadn't chased him, despite the scissors attack.

The intruders couldn't have known whether he'd call the police or not either. All this suggested that he was not dealing with amateurs, as he had already suspected. However, he reminded himself that it wouldn't have been difficult to disappear in such a gigantic building long before the police arrived. All that he was left with were questions, assumptions and the expectation that he would find some answers in the tube.

Chapter 4

First Facts

"And what was in the tube?" Lucia asked, having listened to the story intently.

She was 23, with sun-tanned skin, bright, turquoise eyes and light-brown, almost fair dreadlocks, the longest of them reaching past her shoulder blades. She was wearing thread-bare clothes, but they looked comfortable and practical; jeans, a red t-shirt a couple of sizes too large, and over it a light-brown zip-up hoodie. She also wore heavy leather boots that she only laced up to the top when she had a long way to walk. Her fingernails were cut very short and on each finger – including the thumbs – she wore a plain ring made of stainless steel; the rings emphasised how slender her fingers were. She sat cross-legged on the remains of a wall, with the city disappearing into the night behind her. The light from the small campfire danced across her face and was reflected in the half-full wine glass she was holding with both hands. She had propped her lower arms up on her knees. Next to her, standing on the wall, there was a bottle of red wine.

The fire was burning in the westwork of a mighty cathedral which sat on the spur of a mountain, pointing westwards like the bow of a gigantic ship, heading towards the sea spread out endlessly behind the city. For some incomprehensible reason, the building was hardly over-grown at all; and all around it there were only grasses and flowers.

The north side of the westwork had been seriously damaged at some point in the past, so you could now look out through a gigantic hole over the remaining parts of the wall – which formed a very low counter with 2 metre wide openings on either side of it – providing a view over almost the entire port.

There were two bell towers. The north bell tower hadn't collapsed, but you couldn't quite reach the top via the staircase because of all the damage; the second tower was still intact.

The rubble that must have resulted from the damage to the westwork was nowhere to be seen; someone – with lots of helpers – must have removed it many years or even decades ago.

A few metres away from Lucia, a man was lying on his back next to the fire. His arms were folded behind his head so he could lie more comfortably on the floor as he looked at her. Next to him stood an empty wine glass. His clothing was quite shabby too. He was wearing walking boots, brown trousers with leg pockets and a coarse, grey woollen pullover. He had dishevelled fair hair and an equally dishevelled beard which every now and then he cropped with a pair of scissors or a knife depending on what was at hand. He was 29 and his eyes changed from yellowy-green to yellowy-brown to light orange depending on how the light fell. Not far from him, his guitar was leant up against a wooden chair.

"Construction plans," Cordh answered.

Lucia raised her eyebrows, even though she had already thought that the size of the tube must mean it contained some kind of plans. "Plans of what?"

"Of a gigantic office building."

Lucia took a sip of wine. "And what was it all about?"

Cordh groaned as he sat up – the hard ground was painful. He stayed sitting there, his legs bent, resting his arms on his knees. "If only I knew. A couple of days later, after Gwinard had collected the tube from his locker, seen the contents and cautiously stored everything at his colleague's place, he was visited again. That is how he knew he was being followed, at least some of the time.

This time, someone rang the doorbell. A man presented him with a letter which asked him to call a telephone number within 24 hours and hand over the documents. Apart from a closing threat, it didn't say much at all, so

Gwinard didn't get any closer to finding the answers to his questions."

"Strange story."

Cordh nodded. "It is." He paused for a moment. Then he said: "Before he left, the man promised Gwinard would receive a respectable finder's reward as compensation for the havoc caused in his apartment. Along with the threat, that was enough reason for Gwinard to give the tube back and call the number.

The following day, another man visited. It was the man he had rammed in the face with his scissors as he was escaping. He recognised him because of the now patched up injury. Without saying a word, the man handed over the envelope with the money and disappeared with the tube."

"And what if Gwinard had refused?"

"He would have been killed. He'd also have been killed if he'd held back any of the documents. That's what the letter had said."

Lucia took a sip. "How do you know all this?"

"It's sort of a family story, if you like. My great-great-grandfather was Byrd, the colleague who lived in the same building."

"How long ago was it?"

Cordh pondered for a moment. "It must have happened about 127 years ago. I can't quite remember. I heard the story from my grandfather."

Lucia went over the calculation in her head. "29 years before the *meltdown*."

"That's right." Cordh stood up, reached for his wine glass and headed towards Lucia, where he took the bottle and topped up his glass.

"Did he ever hear back from the people?" Lucia drank the last mouthful of her wine and Cordh topped up her glass with the last of it.

"No." He placed the empty bottle back on the wall. "He and my great-great-grandfather knew how the game had to be played. They had to leave it at that, because back then, if they had informed the police, the information would definitely have got back to those strange guys sooner or later. And they knew what that would have meant."

They paused for a moment, because the man lying a few metres away had moaned briefly.

Lucia was about to get up and check on him, but then he was silent again.

All that one could hear was the fire, and the wind blowing over from the sea, making the cathedral sing through the cracks and gaps in the walls.

"I wonder what was so special about the plans, that they made such an effort to retrieve them." Lucia twizzled her glass and watched the play of light and colour.

Cordh took a few logs from a small pile near the wall and placed them on the fire. "Well, it's a good question." The crackling flames swallowed the energising wood within seconds.

"May I interrupt your little conversation?" a voice asked from the darkness beyond the fire.

Chapter 5

Architecton

Beauford slowly made his way out of the shadows of the cathedral.

"Of course you may," said Lucia and smiled at him.

Beauford was 58. He had curly grey hair reaching down to his shoulders. He wore battered brown shoes, black jeans and a loose dark blue shirt.

What really stood out was that he was wearing glasses. They couldn't quite compensate for his short-sightedness, but it was better than not having any at all. He knew how fortunate he was to have found them, which is why he had connected the sidearms of the glasses with a shoelace, so that he wouldn't lose them easily. He did also own a second pair of glasses in case of an emergency that would hopefully never happen, as they were even weaker.

Cordh removed his guitar from the chair and rested it against the wall next to Lucia. Still standing, he took a sip of wine.

"I must admit, I couldn't help eavesdropping on your conversation, because I woke up and couldn't get back to sleep," said Beauford and sat down on the chair giving Cordh a grateful nod. He crossed his legs and folded his arms.

"The acoustics here mean you can't help but hear everything," said Lucia.

Beauford nodded. "But that's not why I got up. I also have something to add to your conversation."

Lucia and Cordh pricked up their ears.

Beauford explained: "The plans you were talking about belonged to a project commonly known as *The Tower*." He stared into the fire that was blazing in front of him.

"The project was a massive office complex in the shape of a pillar. At first, it was meant to be a triangular construction with corners, but ultimately the shape of a pillar was chosen. As far as I know, this decision was taken simply for aesthetic reasons. The building was meant to look steadfast, majestic and awe-inspiring. There were 48 crescent-shaped channels running down the facade, like the fluting on ancient columns.

In the lower third of the building, the facade arched outwards slightly and then from there to the upper levels it curved inwards again, simply for the look of it. At the top, there was another overhanging section, which made it look even more like a pillar, because it inevitably evoked the impression of a capital atop a column in a temple, as intended. Nothing had been left to chance. At the very top of the building multiple floors ran up to the top in a spiral ending in a glass dome."

Beauford noticed the look of surprise on the faces of the two listeners.

"How do I know all this? You'll find out soon enough, as that's why I got up in the first place."

Lucia sipped her wine without taking her eyes off Beauford as she was captivated by his words, while Cordh nodded and placed his glass on the wall.

"Unfortunately, I can't remember the dimensions or how long it took to build. In the end lots of different types of companies moved into the building. There were meeting rooms and even whole floors which were only used every few months or even years, storage rooms, some the size of warehouses, and apartments which could only be bought and used if you belonged to the right circles."

"Sounds like an ambitious project," said Cordh. He looked through his trouser pockets and retrieved a squashed pack of cigarettes and a lighter. He offered them to Lucia and Beauford. As both declined, he lit a slightly bent cigarette for himself and took a deep drag. He then placed the lighter and the pack next to his wine glass on the wall.

"It certainly was."

Lucia sat up to stretch her back briefly and asked: "Is that another little family story too?"

Beauford laughed. "Yes, and even more so than Cordh's because the architect was my great uncle. And he was directly involved in what Cordh's great-great-grandfather was up to as well, because he provided these strangers with various documents and data storage media. Why it didn't work out when it came to the construction plans, I don't know, as everything else went smoothly."

Lucia frowned and asked: "How did all of that come about anyway?"

Beauford shrugged his shoulders and looked out into the night, which had fallen in the meantime. "One day someone called my great uncle's office and demanded an appointment as they had something important to discuss with him. He first thought it might be about some new work assignment. Two men turned up in the end, both of them very formal, dressed up in suits. Only when they handed over an envelope with photos of his house, his children's houses and their families, as well as pictures of their workplaces, schools, school routes, and the flats belonging to relatives, close friends and their families, did he realise that it was all about something else now."

Cordh took another deep drag on his cigarette and picked up his glass to take a small sip before putting it down again.

"They asked him to hand over all the documents that had anything to do with the project. They didn't even bother to threaten him again once he had seen all the photos."

"And what did they want it all for?" asked Cordh. "And, above all, who were they?"

"That's something my father, who told me this story, couldn't tell me. At some point my great uncle got a message that all the documents were accounted for and that he should just forget about the whole thing. No names were mentioned. It wasn't until now that I knew anything about any delay in handing over the plans in the cardboard tube.

"Maybe one of the contact people dropped out or there was another incident which meant the tube could not be collected. Something must have gone wrong at some point, otherwise the plans would never have been left lying hidden in that backyard for so long, especially under all those strange circumstances."

Beauford glanced over to Cordh. "It's also strange that they managed to find out that Gwinard had the plans."

"Maybe your great uncle had someone keeping an eye on the hiding place to cover his back just in case. They were careless and didn't ask any questions when no-one turned up. And then they mistakenly thought everything had run smoothly. It was never going to be that difficult for that sort of people to find out what had really happened."

"Maybe," said Beauford, who thought this sounded plausible as he didn't really know any of the details. "But it is a good thing that no one assumed my great uncle had gone back on his word. It could all have come to a terrible end."

Lucia was thinking. She took a good swig of her wine. "That is really strange."

"It is indeed," Beauford agreed.

She shook her head slightly. "I don't mean the two stories themselves. I mean, it's so strange that we are sitting here telling each other stories and that your two stories are connected in some way; and that by chance, after so many decades, the descendants of the people in the stories have come together."

Cordh looked over to Beauford. He had to agree with Lucia. If Beauford had not woken up when he did, this connection might never have been discovered and each of them would have continued seeing their own part of the story as a disconnected fragment of the past.

Lucia looked up over her right shoulder to the stars in the sky. "Maybe it's our destiny, and that after so many years, we are all sitting here precisely so that all the different parts can come together again."

Cordh glanced at her quickly: it seemed like she had been reading his thoughts.

"It's a shame we can't save this for posterity," said Beauford.

Lucia nodded, without taking her eyes off the stars twinkling above them. "It is a pity."

"And who knows if it would lead anywhere anyway," said Cordh, to which no one replied.

Beauford looked over at the man lying near the fire. "What about our visitor?"

"I reckon he'll be strong enough to speak to us soon," answered Cordh.

Lucia looked at the sleeping man as well. "I wonder where he comes from."

"We'll find out soon."

Chapter 6

Awakening

Two days later and the man had got enough strength back to be able to walk for a reasonable length of time. What nobody had reckoned with, as became clear after just a few minutes, was that the stranger could not remember anything about his life at all. He told them he didn't know what his own name was, or what had happened just before he turned up in the city. But the strangest thing was that he could not make any sense of the world around him.

The severely emaciated man had an unkempt beard and tousled, light brown hair which had obviously not seen a pair of scissors for years. A scar on the back of his head was surrounded by a mass of dried blood, so the wound had clearly not been inflicted that long ago. Maybe it was also the cause of his memory loss.

It was late afternoon, and the man was sitting on a wooden bench in front of the westwork of the cathedral near where the spur of the mountain came to an end. The bench had been carried out of the cathedral some time ago and placed here – surrounded by leafy trees – overlooking the harbour city.

The edge of this rocky outcrop was secured by the remains of a metal fence hidden beneath the dense undergrowth. Here and there one could see some of the bits of metal, but it was clear that most of it had fallen victim to the ravages of time; however, the wall of climbing plants, thistles and shrubs, including several colourful flowers, formed a natural and no less effective barrier. About 20 metres down the slope below this outcrop, there was a semi-circular terrace – its radius amounting to around 180 to 200 metres – which was home to one of the city's cemeteries.

It was assumed to be the oldest one in the city due to its proximity to the cathedral. A magnificent sea of bushes and flowers waved in the wind punctuated by gravestones and statues which seemed to work like breakwaters to the colourful waves of plants as they blew from side to side in the wind. The spectrum of colours ranged from yellow to orange, then changed in gradual steps between red and violet and on to blue before being transformed into brilliant white; there were even some pink flowers, some deep black ones and some with extraordinary patterns. A multitude of butterflies and bees busied themselves in competition for the sweetest nectar.

At the edge, a row of gigantic columns was lined up along the full length of the terrace, behind them another metal fence lay beneath the undergrowth which had spread itself out to carpet the cemetery; the climbing plants had almost completely swamped the columns, their tendrils winding their way between the gravestones and other plants to gradually disappear over the edge of the spur.

The vegetation covering this extensive slope – part of a long, crescent-shaped chain of hills and mountains, in the distance sloping to the left and the right down to the sea framing the city from one side – flowed seamlessly into the deserted city which nature had been steadily reclaiming over the decades. Grasslands and woods and everything in-between had spread out among the urban canyons and streetscapes, onto and into the ruined houses.

The once lively bustle of the city had given way to the animal world. The greenery had also taken over any vehicles left standing on the streets, and they too were being subjected to the ravages of time – some of them had almost disappeared completely.

In the harbour and along the coast – the sea had eaten its way into the land unhindered – one could make out numerous wrecked ships, some of them sticking up like islands which time had replanted with huge quantities of flowering plants.

Again and again, the man's gaze wandered across this huge city, which must have covered between 100 to 120 square kilometres, constantly discovering new things to

look at. Whereas the northern part of the city was dominated by high-rise buildings, elsewhere hardly any large
buildings got in the way of the view into the distance.

The cathedral was located about 100 metres above sea
level and almost exactly at the apex of the crescent of hills
and mountains. From here to the coast it was approximately
5 to 8 kilometres as the crow flies. A wide road, or what
was left of it, wound its way down the slope, in such wide
loops that the gradient was very gradual.

They had discovered the man, who they reckoned was in
his mid-thirties – although his wild beard and general health
meant this might be well off the mark – during a foray
through the street canyons in the northern part of the city,
where, at the end of his strength, he had dragged himself as
he drifted southwards. He had been in a really bad state and
had stunk to high heaven. They gave him water and bedded
him down on their home-made wagon, which alongside
clothing and freshly gutted fish was also carrying some cans
of food which – in spite of the decades that had gone by –
were perfectly preserved.

After arriving at the cathedral, he had eaten a little and
washed himself down just behind the building, where two
wooden huts had been constructed on an open space below
a fresh water spring. A little stream ran right through the
first cabin, which was closer to the spring, and there were
some shelves to place one's things on while freshening up.
The stream then ran off, disappearing into the greenery on
the side of the mountain.

In the second cabin there was a bathtub, which could be
filled either with cold water or water heated over a fire so
one could just have a wash or lie back and relax.

Around 50 metres away in the nearby woods a little
wooden hut had been constructed, it could easily be moved
to another place once the pit that had been dug underneath it
was full.

Freshly washed and re-clothed the man had said very little
but gratefully ate his fill before giving in to his exhaustion
and sleeping for several days, interrupted only by short

waking periods when he ate, drank and occasionally dragged himself off to the hut in the wood; he had no energy for anything else. Throughout this time, he kept himself to himself and hardly said anything, and even that seemed too much for him.

"I don't know where to start," he admitted and scratched his chin through his full beard. "I have so many questions."

"Why not just ask them one after another," said Lucia, who was sitting on the bench next to the man, who, according to a suggestion from Beauford, everyone now called "Xenos" – the stranger.

He nodded and looked out over the sea to the horizon.

Chapter 7

The Informer

It was a grey, slightly rainy Wednesday.

Verla looked at her watch – 17:48. She picked up her cup of coffee from the small table in front of her and took a sip. Her gaze wandered over to the right and out of the window of the cosy café where she'd been sitting for the last hour.

Her eyes quickly took in the people moving through the shopping street, some of them in a real rush, some just strolling along. And yet again she looked carefully at the window of the second-hand bookshop across the way.

"Why there?" she had asked on the telephone two days ago.

"Because books still exist," was the man's brief answer.

"What's that supposed to mean?"

"Well, people used to think that the digital age would displace all printed works completely. There were some circles who were striving towards that, without question, but they didn't succeed." After a short pause, the man added: "Some people see them as a symbol of hope."

Verla had wanted to say more, but the line was already dead.

"Can I bring you anything else?" the friendly waitress asked.

Verla thought about it. She still had a bit left in her cup, and it would soon be time to go. Her body was already feeling tense with the anticipation, and the butterflies in her stomach were making her feel queasy as well.

"No thanks," she answered. "I'd like to pay now please."

The young woman nodded, smiled and inspected her little notepad. But before she could do the sums, she noticed that Verla was offering her a banknote.

"Keep the change," said Verla, and waited for the waitress to take the money.

"Thanks very much," said the woman, made a note on her pad, put it in her back pocket and took out a little leather purse hanging on a cord attached to her belt. She took the banknote and popped it into the purse. "Do come again soon and hope you have a great day!"

Verla smiled, drank down the last drop of coffee and turned her attention to the street outside again.

The waitress cleared the table and left.

The rain had stopped, she could tell that because people were putting their umbrellas down and looking up to the sky or holding out their hands to check for raindrops.

A gesture of receiving, thought Verla. When the weather is dry, some hope for rain, and on grey days some hope it will stay dry and the sun will show its face.

17:55

"That's when I will go into the shop," the man's voice had said. "No sooner and no later. Either we meet while I'm there, or we don't."

She saw a man stop briefly at the window of the bookshop. He was wearing dark, inconspicuous clothing, like so many other people around him. He bent slightly forwards, as if he was scrutinising a book in the display. Then he turned away and, after glancing at his watch, entered the shop.

Verla hastily grabbed her coat, which was hanging over another chair, and stood up. She put it on and took her handbag from the table. Then she left the café.

As she entered the shop, the little bell hanging over the door rang out and a loud man's voice said: "Have a look around! I'll be here in the back if you want to buy anything or have any questions."

"Thanks!" Verla called back; she felt she had to react so as not to appear like a potential thief.

The second-hand bookshop was dark and cramped. There were shelves everywhere, crammed full of books right up to the ceiling. Here and there notes proclaimed the genres or topic areas to be found in each shelf. Some tables had orderly stacks of books, piled up high to form ramshackle towers. Much of the rest of the floorspace was covered with boxes and crates of books. The aisles formed by all these shelves and books were only wide enough for one person at a time; if anyone wanted to get past, one had to move out of the way by slipping into another aisle.

Verla wandered along the aisles and looked into the niches in each of the rooms, whose real structure and shape were completely hidden by all the books. After some time, she found the man reading a book next to a shelf of works about old cultures. She joined him and picked up one of the books.

"Did we speak on the phone?"

"This would normally be done a bit differently," the man answered without beating about the bush. "But right now, everything is getting out of control." He continued to keep his eyes on the book.

"Do you mean you don't have anything for me?" asked Verla slightly stunned. She gave him a furious sideways look. She had been working on this story for months, and now nothing. If things continued like this, nothing was ever going to come of the investigative novel she wanted to take a step further than just a newspaper article.

"It doesn't matter whether I have anything for you right now."

"Why?" She put the book back in its place without even looking at the title.

The man closed his book and put it on top of one of the piles. "You'll find out soon." He squeezed past Verla without asking. When he was behind her and had to press himself against her to get past, he whispered, almost casually: "Either you'll hear from me or you won't, although that's going to be the least of your worries."

She raised her eyebrows questioningly and wanted to say something, but the man had already gone.

"Can I help you?" asked the bookseller, who had appeared at the end of the aisle. He was quite old, with a bit of a belly and going bald. He had tied his remaining hair into a ponytail and his reading glasses hung from a chain round his neck. He was carrying a stack of books on the way to put them into their rightful places.

"Maybe another time," Verla said frankly and headed off to find the exit.

"Well, you know where to find me and my books," the man said smilingly and went back to his work.

Back on the street Verla noticed that the light rain had started falling again. She quickly looked up and down the street – not a trace of the informer. After glancing at her watch again she joined the crowds of people and headed off to buy a few things she needed.

Chapter 8

The Meltdown

Verla was sitting in a taxi looking forward to a relaxing bath and a glass of wine. She was looking out of the car window watching the lights of the city pass by. It was 23:27.

The traffic lights turned red and the car slowed down and stopped.

She looked through the windscreen and noticed two cars standing in front of the taxi. To the left of her, in the next lane, there was a van and, in front of that, a truck. On the right she saw a tall building stretching high up into the sky. Lights were on in lots of the windows; either people were doing overtime, or the cleaners were hard at work.

The taxi started again and turned off at the second cross-roads to wend its way through the labyrinth of streets to get to her destination.

After about 10 minutes Verla found herself standing at the front door looking for the right key by the light of the lamp above. She unlocked the door, went in and switched on the light in the stairway. She then locked the door behind her and went up the narrow corridor to the stairs. She stopped at her letterbox to take out several letters, as well as that holi-day postcard a friend had promised her; the letters were just bills and advertising. She put the postcard in her handbag and the letters in her shopping bag. Then she went up the stairs.

She was between the second and third floor when the lights went out. A bit annoyed, she continued to climb the stairs carefully, to find that the auxiliary lighting behind the next light switch had also gone. She felt her way along the wall – of course the switch didn't work either – and set off up the remaining steps to get to the fourth floor. At the door to her apartment she had to try practically every key in the lock as she didn't have a lighter or a flashlight, until she finally found the right one and got into her flat, where the lights didn't work either.

"Great," she said to herself and put her handbag and shopping bags down next to the coat stand on a sideboard – she searched through the top drawer hoping to find the flashlight she had put there for just such emergencies.

It felt good when the light from the flashlight lit up the familiar surroundings. She quickly double-locked the door and put the door chain on as well. She then turned around and headed for the kitchen where she took a packet of candles out of one kitchen cupboard and a single candle holder out of another. She found a lighter on the fridge.

After putting the candle into the candle holder and lighting it, she turned off the flashlight and put it on the table. She was just about to take the candle holder to go and get her handbag and shopping bags, when she glanced out of the window. Not quite believing what she saw, she stepped up to the glass to get a better view.

From here she could normally see across the river to the twinkling lights of the city which were usually reflected in the water as well, but apart from the lights of the cars standing in line or slowly moving along the street along the banks of the river, Verla could not see anything out there in the gaping darkness.

What she had initially thought was just a normal power cut, soon turned out to be much more than that. After her neighbour from across the corridor had knocked on her door – an old lady who liked baking cakes and biscuits for her children, grandchildren and the other residents – they joined the other people in the house in the flat of a student, where they were using a battery-powered radio to tune into a radio station that was still broadcasting. This would help them to find out, bit by bit, what was happening.

In fact, the complete power grid had collapsed and not only in their city, but across the whole country – and that also meant that water and gas supplies were down across the board. Practically all means of communication had broken down too; except for a few small radio stations which presumably had their own emergency diesel generators. This slowly developed into a *Network* which could pass on information, but only to those who had some way to receive it. In spite of that, none of the messages they heard was able to say with any certainty what the actual reason was for the enormous chaos that had ensued.

The residents of the building spent the whole of that night listening to the radio. They were so alarmed and scared of missing anything important that it was difficult to sleep. The *Network* broadcast new information every 10 to 15 minutes, slowly revealing just how big the impact of these events was going to be, although every listener could easily see that the power cuts were just the tip of the iceberg.

Chapter 9

Day Zero

"And what happened next?" asked Xenos.

Lucia leant forwards intently, clasping her hands together as she rested her forearms on her knees. "The next day my great-great-grandmother set off to visit her friends and relatives in the city to find out how they were coping.

"There was chaos everywhere she went, and the police just couldn't get it under control. Lots of people were panic buying anything and everything they could get their hands on to hoard away and it wasn't long before the plundering began, which seems to be quite a normal development in such times I'm afraid. To begin with, many were still driving around in their cars but as none of the traffic lights were working, the roads were soon blocked by people trying to get to relatives outside the city where they hoped to sit it out and wait for better times."

Xenos nodded and glanced at Lucia expectantly before turning back to look at the magnificent view again.

"It was only two or three days before the petrol stations had all run out of fuel. The shops were all empty and crime rates shot up. The police were driving through the city with loudspeakers announcing that people should go into lockdown, stay at home and wait it out. That was all they could do. There was no way to get through to the police, ambulance service or the fire brigade if anything happened. So, it was clear that the whole city would gradually sink into pandemonium.

"In the meantime, the news shared by the *Network* was getting worse and worse. Power stations, pipelines, dams and all the essential supply lines had been destroyed in explosions. All the oil rigs and refineries were in flames, as were numerous factories and office buildings. The crops were burning in the fields as well. Another factor in the chaos was that many leading businesspeople and politicians fell victim to attacks, which in turn led to a total lack of any official government. In the face of the circumstances this didn't really have much of an impact on the overall situation though.

"Many planes not forced to return to the airports they had set out from or which had not had to make emergency landings due to the sudden and total collapse of the communication channels, brought the news that this catastrophe was going on in neighbouring countries too. Other planes which had been in the air for 12 or more hours confirmed that the incidents were taking place on a global scale. Similar reports also came in with ships as they arrived in port, sometimes weeks later. Some crews were totally surprised when they dropped anchor in burning harbours and were completely unprepared for what they found after their long journey all alone navigating across the world in the old way using maps, a compass and a sextant."

"How long did they keep the *Network* going?"

"Just a few weeks. It got weaker and weaker as it became more and more difficult to get hold of fuel for the generators. Some stations had help and were able to keep up the information flow to a certain extent. There weren't any alternatives anyway, as practically nobody had access to renewable sources of electricity produced by wind, water or sunlight."

"Yes, suddenly everything was thrown back by decades or even centuries," explained someone who was moving up from behind.

Lucia and Xenos turned round and recognised Forg, who, holding an open tin, was spooning some sort of stew made of potatoes, carrots and onions into his mouth.

"Because the supply of fuel had completely collapsed, it was impossible to do even the simplest things, like planting and harvesting the crops that had mostly been destroyed anyway. But even if that had been successful, it would not have been possible to process and transport it as before." He stopped next to the bench on their left.

Forg was a slim, tough-looking guy, his skin tanned by the wind and weather. Naked from the waist up, he clearly didn't have an ounce of fat on his body. He was wearing white and blue camouflage-style combat trousers and went barefoot.

In spite of just being 39 years old, time was already taking its toll on his face. He had clearly had a very eventful life. Over the years, he had perfected the skill of cutting his own hair and would do so absentmindedly while focusing on some other more important task.

"And it wasn't long before hunger and death accompanied the arguments over stocks of food which were often fought over with weapons," explained Lucia. "The lack of any supplies of medicines and clean water meant diseases soon spread, including some that were thought to have long since died out in most areas, such as the plague."

Forg chewed on his food and left the spoon in the tin which he put down next to Xenos on the bench. "The story of a real apocalypse!" He looked for cigarettes and a lighter in his trouser pockets. "And it was an apocalypse which went on for several decades." He stuck a cigarette in the corner of his mouth, offered Xenos and Lucia one too – only Lucia accepted – and then he lit his and her cigarettes. He took a deep drag and exhaled loudly with obvious satisfaction. He put the box and lighter away again before gazing out over the port. "If you look down there you can see what happened. All technological and medical accomplishments were suddenly of no consequence because the destruction meant that it became impossible to supply all the people in the same way as before and impossible to rebuild the infrastructure. As strange as it sounds, there were too many of us. You might think that many hands mean a large harvest. But their reliance on machines and efficient processes in the past meant only a few were capable of coping with the basics with their own hands and their knowledge. Apart from that, envy, combined with the will to survive of the masses, also meant that this was nipped in the bud from the very beginning; there were no common goals or directions any more, and any new start would have depended on that. Farmers in the middle of nowhere were able to feed their families without too many problems, even though there was no electricity, just like 2000 years before. But cities of 160 million people had no chance and collapsed."

"They caused their own downfall," added Lucia as she flicked ash onto the ground. "All that began 98 years ago when the power outage started. And at some point, the *Network* also disappeared, either because there was no fuel left, the technology failed or because there was nobody left who could receive the news."

Forg took a few steps forward to look over the wall of plants and down to the cemetery. "It wasn't quite as simple as that," he said looking over to Lucia. "But that is mostly true."

"So we are some of the very few survivors," said Xenos, looking questioningly first to Lucia and then to Forg.

"Yes," was Forg's brief reply. He turned to face the others. "People died in droves, and slowly but surely groups formed who fought for survival among the mounds of corpses and decay. These groups ultimately succeeded in wiping each other out too.

"While nature slowly but surely got back to its former strength, the population thinned out drastically. Stories, just like these, were spread by word of mouth just as they had been in the long distant past, and everything was scaled right down. For example, I have no idea what happened on the other continents. But as nobody has appeared to help us get restarted for the last 100 years or so, we can assume that things are the same everywhere. At least we are lucky at these latitudes that we don't get much ice or snow in the winter. In worse-hit areas there are hardly any buildings left to provide shelter. It is said that some of the largest cities have disappeared completely, no two stones left on top of each other to show that anything used to be there."

"Is that why you've come down here from the north?" Lucia wondered, looking at Xenos. She took a drag on her cigarette.

He just shrugged his shoulders sadly, as he really didn't know. He tried to remember but it was no good; his first memories started from when he had joined this group. He gave up and instead turned to Forg: "I wonder how you know all this. Of course, you must have picked up the stories you just mentioned along the way, but where did you get all your knowledge from? For example, about what sorts of fruit you can eat."

"We've all learnt from each other. It's what you grow up with and you find out about this and that from the past or things that you don't really need to survive as you go along. From when you're very young, you learn how to hunt and find water and where you might find something useful to eat or where there's stuff from the olden times."

Xenos looked at the rusty tin.

"The way things were happening back then meant the odd cellar or storeroom would get forgotten, in spite of all the plundering. You wouldn't believe what you sometimes come across and what you can eat and use after so many decades. Clothes and everyday things like a knife or soap. Some things really surprise you. In the end you're dead pleased about anything you find before someone else does." He raised his cigarette as an example. "Down there in the city you can discover all sorts of interesting things. I often wonder what happened here, cos it doesn't really make sense that so much got left behind and wasn't used up." He shrugged his shoulders.

"I know quite a bit, but don't know where I know it from," Xenos started, "and that's why I have a question." Knowing things but not being sure how he knew was a big headache for him.

"Ask away," said Forg and took another deep drag.

Xenos was searching for the right words. "In nature, isn't a high death rate always compensated for by a high birth rate?"

"In nature maybe," Lucia answered, dropping her cigarette end and putting it out with her foot. "But in our case, I guess there was also a lot of infertility and sterility. And most people's sex drive slowly diminished until it was almost completely gone. I can't say how this all connects up anyway. Maybe there's something natural behind it or some sort of poison was released on purpose."

"I've also heard some stories like that," said Forg. "But I've no idea how much truth there might be in them."

"But if you look at it all logically, it does seem there was some sort of plan behind this, something predetermined or a regulating force," said Lucia. "I have a bit of a thing for theories like that."

She then went on to explain some of her theories, some which even Forg had never heard from her before. She began with an unavoidable series of circumstances and natural orders which some sort of higher being had thought up – long before the big bang – and ended up with the idea that probably none of them was actually real.

They talked about it – although Xenos mostly just listened – and shared their thoughts with each other as the sun got closer and closer to the horizon and evening drew in ...

Fragment

He stopped.

He didn't know how long he had been on the road. He couldn't even remember where he had come from and where he wanted to go. It was as if he had got here in a trance and his senses and motor skills had suddenly come back to him.

He was standing in the middle of a large clearing. There were grasses and colourful flowers growing here – mostly in shades of blue and violet but red and orange too – while in the shadows cast by the surrounding trees a sea of ferns and a carpet of moss shared the habitat spread out before him. The tops of the trees were full of twittering birds, crickets chirped in the grass; bees and butterflies flew busily from flower to flower.

He looked up at the sky which was full of fluffy little clouds drifting slowly eastwards. He glanced round but saw nothing except the woods and the fields. So maybe if he just kept walking in this direction, he might find out what his destination was; there must be some reason for his journey.

His stomach was rumbling. His parched throat and dry mouth were also distressing him. His lips were cracked, and his fingers were slightly swollen; he urgently needed water and salt. His sweaty clothes stuck to his skin and he smelt as if he hadn't washed for ages; his greasy hair was all matted and full of things that had got caught up in it as he made his way through the woods and fields. To make matters worse every bit of his beard was itching.

He took a deep breath and continued on his way into the unknown. By the time he reached the first trees at the edge of the clearing he had already settled into a steady jog which drowned out any awareness of the world around him and of his own condition.

Putting one foot mechanically in front of the other, he battled his way through the undergrowth and over fallen trees as the ground slowly started to rise – something he didn't really notice; even hunger and thirst slipped to the back of his mind.

At some point he had to push twigs and branches out of the way to keep heading forwards and soon, half bent over, he burst out of the darkness of the wood. The last branches snapped back into position and it was as if the sunlight, now unhindered by the trees, suddenly woke him up and he came out of his numbed state.

He now looked down on a large city, the dirty grey of the concrete contrasting with the luscious green of the forest. The ridge of the mountain on which he found himself stretched out in a curve to his left, while down to the right he could see the sea and multiple shipwrecks along the coast. Swarms of screeching seabirds soared through the skies.

He suddenly realised there must be water and food some-where down there, so he set off to climb down straight away, not wanting to run the risk of succumbing to weakness while taking a break.

At the edges of the city he passed by the ruins of many homes which rose up from the dense undergrowth of the woods. Then the first signs of asphalt appeared through the grass and slowly but surely more and more remains of the probably once grand city revealed themselves as the vegetation slowly thinned out.

He stopped in front of one of the entrances to the metro. The stairs were covered in a thick carpet of moss, as were the walls and the ceiling further down where the opening into the underground reminded him of a gigantic abyss. In the darkness he could just make out water that had flooded the tunnel, so he turned to continue on his way, completely overwhelmed by all the streets not really knowing which way to go.

A whole wood full of trees had grown out of a high-rise building and a large square was hidden by a field of ivy that had spread out across the ground almost completely taking over the surrounding buildings. Squirrels chased each other through a huge hall covered in moss and ferns where trees so tall looked as if they were holding up the ceiling; climbing plants hung down like a curtain from the branches and swayed backwards and forwards in the wind bearing the fresh, salty taste of the sea. An old fountain was now home to a host of lilac bushes in full bloom looking like a frozen explosion shooting out of the ground. There was lavender everywhere, its heavy scent filling the whole space. In a nearby alleyway, the ground was covered in blue flowers with a sprinkling of red, while creepers hung down from the walls, their origins somewhere high up in the roofs.

And he saw trees growing on a pedestrian bridge, their strong roots reaching down so massively to the ground that it seemed the whole construction would have long since collapsed without them to support it.

He dragged himself onwards through this city of birdsong, downright intoxicated by all the colours and smells, before some people approached him and, without much ado, supported him and gave him some water ...

Chapter 10

Beauford

Lucia clambered over the roots of a gigantic tree standing in the middle of a hotel foyer and stepped out from the shadow of its branches. She was holding a small wooden box which she took over to Beauford who was sitting on a wall about to light a cigarette with his old lighter.

"Not so fast!" Lucia warned him, planting herself in front of him and holding out the box and opening it slowly.

Beauford stuck his cigarette back in the packet in the breast pocket of his shirt as he realised what Lucia had unearthed. He took the box carefully in his hands. "I haven't seen such well-preserved cigars for at least five years."

Lucia sat down beside him on the wall. "I wonder if they still taste any good."

Beauford put his lighter down and inspected the cigars, which all looked perfect.

"Well, we'll soon find out. Where did you find them?"

"In a cupboard down in the cellar under a load of old rubbish," she said. "It was dark and cool down there."

"And being near to the sea means they haven't been too dry either," supposed Beauford.

Lucia glanced over to her right, where some way away she could see her cart on which, in addition to a bucket of water and the freshly caught and cleaned fish, there were all sorts of things she had found on her tour today. The others had all swarmed out to search the buildings in the street for whatever useful things they might find.

Behind the wall, almost completely covered in moss, there were some huge bushes with grand, sweetly smelling flowers. The pavement in front of the wall was just a pile of gravel now, almost unrecognisable through the grass, and most of the street itself had turned into a meadow, with hardly any flowers breaking up the green expanse.

Beauford had carefully taken out a cigar and placed the wooden box on the soft moss to his left. "No sign of crumbling." He inspected the cigar closely from all angles. Its smell was subtle.

Lucia was already somewhere else in her thoughts, looking up at the intense blue of the beautiful, cloudless sky.

"Shall we give it a go?" asked Beauford with a big grin, checking that the others were nowhere to be seen.

Lucia nodded and grinned as well, as the situation was slightly childish; after all it was a little secret for them to keep to themselves.

"Not much can go wrong except it crumbling to bits or tasting awful," said Beauford, as he made a little cut at the closed end with his pocketknife, lit his lighter and took a few puffs to get the cigar going. He thought how wonderful it would have been if there had been a box of matches in the cigar box too.

"I don't know why, but I never really got round to asking you how you ended up here," said Lucia as she took the cigar to try it.

Beauford toyed with the lighter, twisting it this way and that, and looked up the street to the left, where a copse of trees at the end blocked the view of the wrecked ships in the harbour. "That I can tell you: ever since I was born, I had been constantly changing between groups, until I met my wife and stayed in her group. About three years ago we decided to set out on our own, as there seemed to be a bit too much infighting in the group."

"What were the arguments about?"

"Oh, there was always someone who wanted more than the others, supposedly because they were worse off, or because they deserved more, and some felt the need to get recognition and insisted on speaking their mind whenever important decisions had to be made. Towards the end you could never be sure whether someone might go crazy and murder somebody."

"That doesn't sound so great," said Lucia handing back the cigar. She thought the aroma was pleasant enough and wondered whether it had survived the passing of time or whether time had actually been the cause of it.

"I mean, just look around you," said Beauford as he demonstratively looked around himself. "Times are tough, and you have to decide whether you can rely on each other or if you are better off on your own." He took another puff on the cigar. Finding cigarettes was not easy, so a find like this was like a gift of the gods.

Lucia nodded and looked over to the cart in the distance, which Cordh had just loaded something onto, before briefly waving to her and disappearing back into a house.

"In the middle of last year, I woke up one morning and straightaway noticed that something was not quite right." He paused briefly. "She'd died in her sleep. I don't know why, as she didn't have any injuries or a cold or any other illnesses that you could actually see." He looked over to Lucia. "If there's nobody around who has an idea about these things, it's just a matter of luck, as you can't see what's happening to people inside. Either you survive an infection or you don't. For example, you'll never even know if you have a congenital heart defect. The times we had medicine like that are long since gone."

Lucia nodded silently.

"I buried her in a meadow, carved her name into a piece of wood and rammed it into the ground." He inspected the cigar. "I don't even remember where it was. I stayed a few days to mourn her passing before continuing on my way. Over the following weeks and months I always gave a wide berth to any groups I spotted. I had been carrying a gun since we had set off which had helped me a couple of times when we came across animals, but it suddenly stopped working. Luckily, it happened when I was just trying to shoot something to eat and not having to protect my life. I chucked it into the sea."

He puffed away on the cigar and then handed it to Lucia.

"And at some point you ended up here."

"One evening, at dusk, with the light disappearing fast, I was walking through the streets looking for a suitable place to spend the night. I looked up and discovered the cathedral high up over the city, because I saw the light of a fire."

"And this time you didn't give it a wide berth," Lucia surmised and puffed on the cigar.

Beauford nodded. "I don't really know why not. Maybe I'd been keeping everything and everyone at bay for too long, or I was just too tired to think straight. Or maybe it was hunger that subconsciously pushed me up here, because a fire means warmth, company and usually food. Anyway, I dared myself to climb up to the cathedral where I met Forg, who was sitting next to the fire. He just looked up briefly from his book. On the other side of the fire Cordh was fast asleep under some blankets. We didn't speak a word all night. Forg offered me water and some root vegetables which I roasted in the fire."

A sparrow landed on the wall some distance away and looked over at them suspiciously before picking at the insects in the vegetation.

Lucia and Beauford looked over at the bird without moving.

The sparrow suddenly flew away.

"At some point he gave me a blanket and lay down for the night. He obviously just hoped I wasn't a thief or a crazy murderer."

Lucia took another puff and handed the cigar back to him.

"The next morning the three of us introduced ourselves."

"Are you coming?" shouted Cordh from far away, waving his arms.

Lucia waved back to signal that they had heard him. As she jumped off the wall, she said: "I still think it's strange that our group came together right here at this place. The population is shrinking, the cities are deserted and collapsing, and the planet is getting greener while we are living right here and now, regardless of any other groups that might be around somewhere.

Beauford took another puff, put the lighter away and jumped down from the wall as well. "Just wonder where this will take us in our lifetime." He took the wooden box and set off with Lucia to catch up with the others who had already set off slowly with the cart.

Lucia saw Sydell walking a few metres behind the cart, which Cordh was pulling. Forg was walking next to him. They seemed to be talking to each other.

Sydell; it was difficult to work this woman out. She was very quiet, avoided almost everyone and behaved like a shy deer, always watching everyone and everything, assessing the situation and weighing up what to do next. She took part in everything the group did, but was still very independent. She always slept slightly away from the rest of them – but in sight of Lucia. She was 43, slim, very fit and looked tough, determined and quite militant in a way. This last characteristic was emphasised by the way she kept her hair very short with a combat knife, and her weather-beaten skin – if you didn't know any better, you might easily take her for Forg's partner as they looked so similar.

"Maybe this is like an oasis for us, where we can all get our strength back," said Lucia, taking the cigar again and puffing on it.

"That's possible," agreed Beauford, happily breathing in the scent of all the flowers, some hidden, some visible, unfolding their magnificence as their sweet fragrance combined with the dreamy smell of the fresh sea air. "You just can't get an overview of the whole situation. A hundred years ago there were so many sources of information that you could easily find out what was happening elsewhere. Who can say how much our average life-expectancy has changed since everything collapsed? In the end questions like that are irrelevant, because everything changed. In the past, people searched for their own meaning of life through art, in their work or by creating things. Or by starting a family. And now? All of that became more and more unimportant and now we just think about surviving and only occasionally do we wonder about things from the time before *Day Zero* or are delighted by a relic of those long-gone times. But you do have to keep in mind that we don't really have any direct connection to that past as we were born much later. And it's impossible to learn from the mistakes of the past because they were all washed away, buried under all the plants or at least they are about to disappear – in the end they'll disappear from our thoughts too. And not forgetting that there is hardly anyone left who, even theoretically, could do it any better."

Beauford noticed that he was digressing but didn't stop there.

Lucia, saying nothing, took a few puffs on the cigar and handed it on to Beauford.

"The question of what tomorrow will bring is as old as humanity itself. And because it is not possible to answer that question with any certainty, we just keep on going. I think we passed the point of no return, where we started heading unerringly towards the end, ages ago. Decades ago in fact." He puffed away.

"Just like with our knowledge, which we can't even expand by looking things up, because most sources have long since turned to dust. But in the end, it doesn't really help you if you know how to calculate the strength of a building, if you eat poisonous berries."

"Quite sad when you think about it," said Beauford.

"Maybe this is an oasis for sharing ideas as well."

Beauford nodded. After a few metres he stopped, squatted and put the cigar out cautiously on the ground before laying it carefully back in the box, while looking up briefly to keep an eye on the others in front.

Lucia watched everything with a smile.

It was impossible for him to hide the box on him anywhere, as he realised. It was too big for that. But he could try to put it secretly under his pullover which was lying on the cart. It was worth a try.

They then strolled calmly along behind the others until they caught them up. Soon after that, they came across a man who looked like he had had a long, arduous journey behind him ...

Retrospective

The constant battle among the groups for the remaining resources slowly wore people down – or even destroyed communities completely. Over the decades, fights and disease meant that even the largest groups only consisted of around 50 people: there were reports of some larger mergers but it was difficult for anyone to find any real evidence. It was also said that some weaker groups had joined forces to improve their chances of survival and to defend themselves against possible enemies. But, with the prospect of everything coming to an end looming over them, the battles and the never-ending search for food meant new settlements were never founded. Groups of people wandered around like nomads, isolated from everything, as if they were living under a glass dome. Although there was some exchange when they came across other groups, there was no constant or regular contact, due to the unstable life the groups all led.

In addition to knowledge and the latest news, they also shared tips about important places – such as fresh water sources – and possible dangers which might lie on the way. Goods of all kinds were traded, because apart from gold, silver or other precious metals and precious stones, there was hardly anything remaining that could serve as an accepted form of payment – and it might lead to greed, robberies and murder. High value was placed on things that had survived from before *Day Zero*, such as clothing, stimulants, tools and weapons.

Another important aspect was the things which people could produce themselves. These ranged from cultivated and dried herbs, tobacco goods and alcoholic drinks, to clothing, shoes, backpacks and other necessities of daily life, such as wooden beakers and bowls, bottles made of leather or wood, knives and simple mechanical lighters. Not many people had the skills to work with metal and glass, which is why such products – like glasses, lenses and tools – had a much higher value.

Working the fields was pretty much an exception due to the risk of attacks, as was breeding animals. Any livestock, which were also good trading goods, generally moved along with the groups as this was safer.

As the groups got smaller and fewer, the more seldom they came across each other and the more lonely life became; in quiet moments people wondered why they should go to all the bother when there was no real hope of a better life, remembering how life had been for their ancestors and the opportunities they had had back then. Maybe, the answer was just over the horizon.

Chapter 11

Forg

For several days, the group had been sheltering in an overground bunker, waiting for an end to the rain. The colossus of reinforced concrete, completely overgrown with moss and creepers, rose from the remains of a city which, as they had discovered on their reconnaissance tours, had little to offer; all that was left amidst the desolate ruins were a few fruit trees and animals that were all but impossible to kill in such surroundings. From the blackness that was scorched into the walls, it was clear that at some point a huge fire had raged and devoured everything.

Forg, who had returned from a trek wet and frozen, was drinking tea to warm himself up. Having changed into dry clothes, he sat huddled in a blanket in one of the chambers that had been chosen for living quarters, listening as the wind whistled and roared through the bowels of the hulking edifice. Around him, some members of the group were sleeping, while noises from elsewhere in the bunker hinted at livelier things going on. Here, in the stuffy chamber, some candles provided a gentle glow.

Through the gloom the iron door suddenly squeaked opened a crack. A man stepped in halfway and spoke in a hushed whisper: "A group has arrived and is asking for shelter. About 25 to 30 of them, some of them women!" He vanished again, his footsteps mingling with the other sounds that animated the darkness.

Indifferent, Forg finished off his drink, as he was far too exhausted to get up and join in, stuffed the aluminium cup into his backpack, adjusted it a little, then lay his head on it and stretched his limbs with a yawn as some men left the room. The insulated mat on which he lay was not comfortable, but it served its purpose. He reached for the second blanket beside him, covered himself with it, turned onto his right side and took a deep breath, only to fall into a deep slumber ...

He was woken by a sound. As he opened his eyes, he saw in the flickering light of the candles a shadow bending over one of the dozing forms close by. A moment later, the shadow made a jerky movement, accompanied by the squelch of flesh and a brief twitch of the person on the floor; something was dripping. The shadow straightened up, looked around, took a few steps in Forg's direction and bent over another unwitting soul. Again, a rip and a squelch; but this time, Forg's nose also picked up the distinctive smell of blood.

He drowsily closed his eyes for a moment and opened them again. There were two more sleeping bodies between himself and the shadow. In the background he could make out the closed door. He remembered that he had fallen asleep with his back to the door. How long ago could that have been? Here, in the heart of the bunker, there were no gun slits that would have revealed whether the sun had yet risen. He also wondered whether he alone was awake; was everyone else asleep or were they too watching, frozen?

The wind howled an eerie song as the shadow rose again.

Forg had to make a decision. Should he jump up and make a run for it? Would he even be able to dodge the shadow and escape unscathed? Or should he lie still and strike at the last moment? The threat was almost upon him, as the questions turned to options as to how he might overpower the shadow without becoming acquainted with its weapon. Whether this was a knife or perhaps a shard of glass, he could not tell.

Another cut.

Forg did not know who had just breathed his last. But he knew that he did not intend to meet his own end at any price and, above all, not without a fight. He could not think of any object within reach that would serve as a weapon – and even if there was something, there was no time to search for it the murky gloom.

The shadow straightened up again, looked around and appeared to listen attentively for signs of movement. It then took two sideways steps and looked down at the sleeping figure beside Forg.

Without wasting another thought – and thus time – Forg tensed his muscles, tore the blankets from himself and, with all his strength, kicked outwards in an arc, his right leg hitting the shadow in the back of the left knee. The shadow buckled, lost its balance and tumbled backwards. Forg leapt up, let out an unintelligible yell and rushed headlong for the door.

As he hurried downwards and neared the exit of the over-ground bunker, the bellows of those he had left behind, awoken by the commotion, became fainter. He ran through the darkness, which was interrupted here and there by faint candlelight emanating from some of the chambers. He could make out several bodies, all of whom had most probably died in their sleep, for a ruckus would have stirred him from his sleep much sooner.

Eventually he stepped out into the night, where he was greeted by icy rain and a biting wind. He paused for a moment to get his bearings, but behind him he could hear hasty footsteps approaching. Whether it was help on the way, a fellow survivor from the bunker, or the shadow, he did not care to wait and find out. Instinctively, Forg ran leftwards to the corner of the bunker and there turned left again – at this point he was already soaked to the skin. The lashing rain, he hoped, would conceal his movements; if someone were in pursuit, this would prove an invaluable advantage.

Through the inky darkness, the irregular flashes of an imminent thunderstorm provided just enough light to make out the surroundings. He ran and staggered, brushed against the billowing undergrowth that rose up around him, and felt lost as rarely before in his life. He could hear nothing but the rain, which almost completely drowned out his breathing and the sound of his steps on the soft, muddy ground.

His plan was to reach the next corner and from there continue running in a straight line until he had no more strength. He knew he had to gain as much distance as possible.

Suddenly he stumbled over a person cowering on the ground and fell headlong into the mud. He felt water and earth in his nose and mouth. Spurred on by his experiences so far that night, he kicked at the cowering figure; at the same time, he scrambled to his feet and turned around, panic-stricken.

When Forg had regained his bearings, he saw that the person had backed away and was crouching against the wall of the bunker. Whoever it was, he was evidently not out to kill him.

"Leave me alone!" cried the young man. He groped around for a rock that he might use as a weapon.

"If we don't get out of here right now, we're both done for," Forg replied forcefully over the wind and rain and the advancing thunderstorm. He would have spoken even louder but for the lethal risk of attracting attention.

The man stood up; he was aware of the danger.

Without hesitation, they both ran towards the corner and from there continued straight ahead, pausing for nothing and no one. Within moments, they had vanished into the stormy night.

Chapter 12

Cordh

"What did you do once you got outside?" asked Lucia.

"I just wanted to get away," explained Cordh, "and then I stumbled and fell to the ground!"

"And just a few seconds later, I did the same," added Forg. "Maybe that's why we're still alive today. Who knows what would have happened to us if we hadn't bumped into each other."

Cordh nodded silently. He would have been able to escape, but now he couldn't say for sure whether he would have survived for so long all on his own.

"When was that?" Xenos wanted to know.

"About two years ago," answered Cordh.

Forg nodded. "That sounds right. I can't say exactly which month it was, but it was definitely in the summer. I know that because I had spent the previous winter further up in the north. The further south you get, the harder it is to estimate time, unless you've made some notes, because the individual seasons start to vanish, as you know."

"Doesn't anyone keep a diary?" asked Xenos.

"I do," said Lucia, "but I usually just cross off the days. More for myself than anything else, as it's not important to keep time precisely anymore. Even though you do sort of count days off in your head, to help remember special events and to put them in context, but you don't really need to. In the end one day here or there doesn't really matter. Before the *meltdown* practically all aspects of life were dominated by timekeeping. Now it is just either day or night. You just have to observe nature closely. The rest is not really important."

They were sitting on some moss-covered steps which were completely overshadowed by the houses on either side and led down to a square with a huge hole in the middle where the metro tunnel beneath it had caved in. Creepers and plants hung down into the crevice where, if you got near enough, you could see down to the water which had filled up the tunnel. From the other end of the square, more steps led further on down to the remains of the former harbour promenade, beyond which you could see the sea glistening in the light. All around, the tall ruins reaching into the sky formed a sort of wind tunnel blowing cool air up through the streets and alleyways providing a pleasantly refreshing breeze accompanied by waving plants and the calls of the sea birds.

Lucia sat on Forg's right-hand side and Xenos to his left, while Cordh sat a few steps below Lucia: they were all looking down at the square in front of them. Beauford was just a few steps behind the group next to the wall of the house on his right. Sydell had made herself comfortable a bit further away leaning her back on the wall of the building on the other side of the steps. In spite of being so spread out, they could all hear each other fine.

Beauford looked around. He wondered how the world must have sounded in the past with all the machines and people. Had there been anywhere where you couldn't hear planes flying overhead?

He looked to the others: "I don't know if any of you have noticed, but this is the first time that all six of us have sat down together. Otherwise at least one of us has always been missing, or not all of us were actually sitting down." They all glanced up at him as if to make sure that it was really true. The silence spread around them.

"And what happened next?" Xenos asked after some time had gone by.

"We ran," said Cordh, who was looking across the square towards the sea. "I don't even remember how long we ran for. At some point we noticed that dusk was settling in and it wasn't raining anymore. Our clothes were almost dry again as well."

Beauford lit up a cigarette, took a deep drag, leant back on the steps and exhaled with obvious pleasure.

"We had to make a decision, so we set off towards the west," explained Cordh, who wanted to tell his part of the story now. "Forg's group had originally wanted to go east and, until they met up, mine had wanted to go south west. After the events of the night we didn't even consider going back to the bunker even though we were now in the middle of nowhere and had nothing but our clothes. In fact, it would have been quite difficult to work out where we had come from as we had more or less headed off blind. So, we just went west.

"While we walked, we talked about what had happened.

"After my group had arrived, I'd organised somewhere to put my head down later and just wanted to be alone for a bit, so instead of lying down straightaway, I had something to eat and drank the hot tea someone offered me, then went outside of the bunker again even though it was still raining. Lucky for me, because that's what saved my life."

Everyone listened eagerly to his words and wondered why they hadn't sat down like this before to listen to each other's stories.

"I was standing near the entrance and overheard someone from my group talking to someone from the other group."

"Could you hear what they were talking about?" asked Beauford from behind him as he took another drag on his cigarette.

Cordh shook his head. "No, I didn't really think too much about it. They then went into the bunker and I followed them a few minutes later, and I immediately noticed that the atmosphere had changed. I can't really say why."

It was as if everyone was holding their breath to see what had happened next.

"I wanted to go into one of the recreation rooms which had been assigned to us to see if I could get anything else to eat. On my way over I heard some steps and a quiet sound. Somebody was walking around, and I heard this sound again. I slipped over to a door which was standing open and peeped inside. Three of the people from my group were lying on the ground. I could see by the light of the candles that were still burning that they had been shot in the head. That's obviously what the strange sound had been."

"... a silencer ..." Lucia guessed in a very quiet voice.

Cordh nodded. "I didn't think twice and just stormed out of the bunker." He glanced over at Forg. "It was just after that, that we literally bumped into each other and made our getaway."

Suddenly, Sydell stood up. With a slight nod in Xenos' direction she said: "Your newcomer is up to no good, you know, I can smell it."

Everyone looked up at her with surprise.

"You don't have to look so shocked, you damned bastard," she said coolly. Turning to the others: "If I were you, I would never turn my back to him." She looked over at Xenos again. "And if you get too close to me, I will kill you."

With these words and under the gaze of the others, she headed up the steps and soon disappeared from the street as she turned a corner to the right.

"What's got into her?" asked Beauford, obviously irritated, and turned back round to the others.

"Honestly?" asked Lucia and looked him in the face.

Beauford nodded and took another drag on his cigarette.

"I think something terrible happened to her and that turned her into what she is today. I reckon she's basically a loner, and there must have been a reason for that."

Nobody else commented on this. It was clear that all of them had survived so far; that meant they were all able to stand up for themselves whatever type of person they were.

What none of them let on though was that Sydell had said something out loud that all of them had been thinking for a while even if they hadn't said anything to the others. What if Xenos had been putting it all on and did know what he was called and what had gone on before? What if he knew all too well what he was doing? On the other hand, the terrible state he had been in when they found him would have been a masterstroke of disguise; nobody could play that so convincingly and still be in such a bad physical state. It wouldn't have made any sense to starve himself or not to drink anything just so that he would be found in such a condition; not in this area. And several days had gone by now without anything happening, even though Xenos would have had plenty of chance.

Without actually discussing it, Sydell's warning meant they all decided to watch out for themselves and the others even more than usual.

"What happened next?" asked Beauford to break the silence, which had certainly conjured up a strange atmosphere. He took a last drag on his cigarette, stubbed it out next to him and left the end on the ground.

"We wandered around that region for ages, without staying in any one place for too long," explained Cordh. "We did come across a few people, but we always kept ourselves to ourselves. We kept out of trouble and avoided people who seemed strange in any way. We just relied on our gut feelings.

"Nowadays we are better company than we were 2 years ago. Back then any sort of sitting around with other people would have been out of the question. And I reckon, based on my own experience, that there might be something in what Sydell is on about, and that she experienced something to make her so careful. But that is just by the by."

Cordh wondered what he had actually wanted to say.

"At some point we had to change the route we had planned to take because we came upon a wide river that meandered its way through the countryside, and at that point it was just impossible to get across to the other side. So, we decided just to follow the course of the river. We did manage to get over to the other side later on, but it wouldn't have made any sense to head back upriver just to continue where we had been blocked off before. That's why we kept on in the same direction. At some point we got to the coast and followed it southwards and that eventually got us to where we are now. About eight months ago, I guess. And we were instinctively drawn up to the cathedral from where you can look over the whole area, as you know."

"And six months ago, some old man showed up and joined you," Beauford joked.

Forg nodded. "Three months after that Sydell ..."

"... and two months ago, it was me," said Lucia.

"And then just a couple of days ago the newcomer arrived," said Xenos, who was obviously very upset by the situation.

"Don't worry about Sydell," Forg suggested. "Just try and avoid her as much as possible. That shouldn't be too difficult."

"I'm afraid I can't prove that I can't remember anything," said Xenos and sighed. "I would feel better if I at least knew where I come from and what brought me here. But none of you can look inside my head to convince yourselves that I'm not lying."

"Maybe it will all come back to you with time," said Lucia, trying to cheer him up a bit. "Maybe it's just temporary." She thought about the scar on the back of his head.

Xenos shrugged his shoulders.

They remained sitting on the green steps for a while listening to stories from Forg and Cordh about the first few weeks they had spent in the city, before they all headed back up to the cathedral together, where they met Sydell who had been sitting in the shade of a tree gazing out over the city from this vantage point. The sun was starting to go down, washing everything in a magical, golden light, while a refreshing breeze from the sea wafted over them.

Chapter 13

Lucia

There was an oppressive atmosphere. A blanket of clouds concealed the blue of the sky, lending the day a truly gloomy feeling. It was really humid as well, with scarcely the hint of a breeze to provide even temporary relief. It was a struggle to overcome the torpor and escape the clutches of boredom.

While the others set out for a wander around the city, scouting for anything that might be of use, Lucia had invited Sydell to join her on a little mission of their own. This would, Lucia reasoned, be an opportunity to chat one-on-one, to glean a couple of stories from the loner and thus establish a rapport with her.

"Have you ever noticed how some places just seem to be in total harmony?" asked Sydell, as they arrived at a spot where two roads crossed. It was impossible to tell whether it had once been an intersection or a roundabout. Ruins were all that remained of the buildings, reclaimed by nature to varying degrees.

Tender grass grew everywhere, and at the centre three strong sycamores had sprung up, towering high and almost spanning the space with their canopy.

"The grass seems greener, and the air cleaner, the trees more majestic," she explained, stopping to look at the square which, due to the sultry haze, barely hinted at its former glory.

"I've had that feeling before too," agreed Lucia. "Not very often, but when I do, it's like seeing something for the very first time. I suddenly feel hyper-aware, as if refreshed."

Sydell crouched down and ran her fingers over the tips of the blades of grass. "So do I. It gives me a sense of peace and comfort."

Lucia glanced down at Sydell and said nothing.

"It must have been strange back in the days when people wondered what colour to paint their homes. Or which furniture to put in them, which plants to grow by the window." She straightened up again. "When people looked at paintings and photographs just for beauty's sake."

"I like to do that too – I mean, looking at beautiful things and sceneries," replied Lucia. "Mostly places like this because anything else is rare." She looked around at her surroundings.

Sydell nodded. "It's like a primitive instinct that forces you to pause and take it all in. It must be something like that if it happens again and again, that you stop in your tracks and look around yourself in wonder and awe."

They continued walking towards the trees.

"By the way, I know exactly why you asked me to come out for a walk with you," Sydell announced. She smiled as she spoke.

"That's not the only reason," protested Lucia. "We're the only women in the group and I reckon it can't do any harm if we do something together, just the two of us." She laughed. "And of course, I want to get to know you better." Had she seriously thought Sydell would take her invitation at face value? She shook her head inwardly.

"Then maybe we should start by telling each other how we got here," suggested Sydell as she stopped beside one of the trees and pressed her hands onto the flaky bark, contemplating its coarse structure.

"Sounds good," agreed Lucia and sat down cross-legged in the soft grass. Since it had been her idea, she felt obliged to take the first step and tell her story. Perhaps this would help to put Sydell at ease.

Sydell glanced around her briefly and sat down facing Lucia, wrapping her arms around her drawn-up legs.

"For as long as I can remember, I travelled alone with my parents," Lucia began, tearing off a blade of grass. "It's as if, by choosing solitude, parents want to shelter their children from all the bad things. Over time we got to know a few other families and they lived exactly like we did."

Sydell nodded silently and watched as Lucia toyed with the blade of grass.

"They taught me all kinds of things. Often, when we met other people, we'd share what we knew so that each could benefit from the chance encounter. We would roam from place to place and follow some of the advice. You just had to get by as best you could." She looked up briefly. "You know what I mean, like all of us did."

Sydell nodded again. She was not tempted to interrupt Lucia's story, sensing from the tone of her voice that she too was about to hear things that none of the others knew; perhaps with good reason, for sharing knowledge makes you vulnerable and that could be dangerous.

"One day, my parents went off to talk. I thought nothing of it as I sat by the campfire, watching a rabbit on the spit. It was my job to make sure it didn't burn. They came back a short time later and my father announced that we would be changing our route. He didn't want to tell me any more than that. It was to be a surprise.

"Two weeks later my mother fell ill. Pneumonia. She became weaker and weaker, and nothing helped." Lucia paused. "One of the many prices we pay when you compare these times with stories of the past. Back then, people in most parts of the world had access to doctors."

She dropped the blade of grass and picked another.

"We searched for a suitable place where we could stay for a while, where my mother could rest and we could care for her," continued Lucia. "My father built a shelter at the edge of a forest where she would be warm and dry. At some point she wanted to take a nap. My father and I went looking for firewood to make tea from herbs we'd collected. But when we returned, we realised that she wasn't going to wake up."

Tears welled in Lucia's eyes as she spoke.

"We stayed with her until the next morning, drinking tea and sharing memories of the times we'd had. Then we buried her right there and set off around noon.

"Over the next few days, I noticed that my father was also losing his strength. He'd always been a mountain of a man, but before long his features began to change, and the shine disappeared from his eyes. It was as if he secretly wanted to go to my mother, although he would never have admitted it to me even if I'd asked him. But somehow, I understood and still do.

"He tried to hide it. He would weep at night when he thought I was fast asleep, but I could feel his energy and will to survive gradually leaving him. Then, one morning I woke up and he was gone. He'd left me a letter in which he asked me to forgive him and wrote that I should follow the setting sun as far as the sea and then move northwards. There I would find the destination of the journey we'd begun together."

"I assume your destination was the city," said Sydell.

Lucia nodded and looked at her as she wiped the tears from her eyes before going on: "He explained that he'd heard about the city long ago and apparently few people had gone in search of it. Why not, he didn't know.

"And so, I set off. I had no choice. I didn't know where to look for my father, but I knew he'd gone to join my mother. The letter also contained survival advice. Much of it I already knew from him and my mother, but some of it was new to me. He must have been writing it secretly and planning all this for quite some time.

"By the number of dashes in my journal, I must have been on the road for about nine weeks before I arrived here."

"Do you still have your father's letter?" asked Sydell.

Lucia threw the blade of grass to her side. "No. All my belongings got drenched in a storm. There was nothing left of the letter, so I had to throw it away. Sadly."

"We're all stranded somehow," observed Sydell, "like castaways on an island."

"You're right," agreed Lucia and lay back in the grass. She looked up at the canopy hanging heavy and listless above them. The cold dew soaked through her clothes and onto her skin. Her trousers were already damp from sitting down, but she didn't mind. "And what's your story?"

"Much worse," replied Sydell succinctly.

Chapter 14

Sydell

"As for me, my family lived in a house in the middle of nowhere. My parents had been part of a group that came across this house, and the two of them decided to repair it and settle there, together with my father's mother and my mother's elder sister. At some point my brother and sister were born, then me. We had everything we needed. There was a pond nearby fed by a little stream, a forest and enough land to grow things like tomatoes, cereals, corn, potatoes, cucumbers, peppers, carrots and various herbs. We'd brought some of the seeds with us on our travels and the rest were given to us by members of the group as a farewell gift. We got our water from the stream and a small well beside the house. We rarely had meat as we could only hunt with traps and we didn't catch much. But we were happy with our lot.

"Over the years, groups or lone travellers passed by from time to time, and their tales of adventure were a welcome change. But the bitter struggles we heard about convinced us we had best remain where we were, far away from any trouble.

"Everything changed when I was 13. My sister was 19 and my brother 17. Our grandmother had died two years earlier and our aunt had barely left her bed for weeks, as she was growing old and weak.

"One night, I woke with a start. I was sleeping in the attic, which my father had converted into a small bedroom as the family had grown larger. My aunt slept on the ground floor and everyone else on the upper floor.

"I heard a loud scream and the sound of several people charging into the house. I was wide awake in an instant and knew instinctively that I had to get to safety no matter what. I ran to the window on the gable end, but I could hear several men outside. Not directly below the window, but around the corner to the left, somewhere near the front door. I knew at that point that I wouldn't be able to run away without being caught, even though I knew I could climb down from the window without any difficulty; I'd often dangled myself from the windowsill and dropped down without ever hurting myself. I couldn't hide inside the house either. I could hear crashing as they turned everything over. So, I quietly opened the window, climbed onto the sill and, holding onto the window frame with one hand, I leaned outwards to grab the eaves with the other.

"I've no idea how, but I managed to pull myself up onto the roof without being noticed. I crawled along the ridge to the chimney and slid carefully onto a flat part of the roof to one side of the house. I lay down flat on my stomach and waited. There were no windows in the roof, so I knew I was quite safe up there. There was a full moon and a cloudless sky, but I'm convinced the night gave me extra protection. Or maybe I was just lucky that the intruders only watched the front of the house.

"I lay there on the roof and had to listen as my family screamed and begged for their lives. There was nothing I could do. I knew what they were doing with my sister and that they were slaying the others, because the screams became quieter and then they fell silent. And all the while I prayed that no one would discover me.

"Shortly after dawn they moved on. To this day, I don't know how many of them there were. I stayed where I was until nightfall, for fear that they may return at some point during the day and I might run into them by chance. Then I climbed down by hanging from the lowest part of the roof and dropping myself down the last two metres. As I said, I'd had plenty of practice. I ran into the house, grabbed a few essentials, started a fire in the main room and waited outside until everything was engulfed in flames. Then I set off.

"It felt like I was dreaming, nothing felt real. I'd tried to avoid seeing the horrors inside the house, but I couldn't because there was blood and devastation everywhere. The images burned themselves into my memory alongside the screams.

"I can't say how long I travelled before I could begin to think clearly. A week? Two? Three? I ended up surviving on my own for the next 30 years, dealing swiftly with anyone who felt the need to get too close. I lost count of the number of people I killed or disfigured in self-defence. I don't care though. It was them or me.

"Then, about three years ago I heard of this city on the west coast. Some people had been there and said great things about it. But I soon forgot about the story until one morning, when I woke up and remembered, and decided to go and find it for myself.

"This is where my story meets yours because it's obviously the same city your father had heard of. A strange coincidence, considering how few of us there are here. I wonder why no one ever settled here. Maybe people have only ever been passing through. Or could it be the mountains people are afraid of? I must admit, I feel it too sometimes: trapped between the ocean and the mountains, we're like sitting ducks.

"In any case, I arrived three months ago, and I can tell you, I feel better here than anywhere else ... *since what happened*. It's not that I trust you all absolutely, but I don't feel any immediate threat from you either. That doesn't apply for the new one, mind you. I'll be keeping an eye on him – I don't trust him one bit.

"Well, that was my story."

Chapter 15

Conversation at Night

Flashes of lightening repeatedly lit up the dark night sky, while the howling storm and heavy rain whipped their way inland; the sinister rumble and loud claps of thunder almost went unnoticed. The wind whistled threateningly through the cracks and holes in the roof and stonework of the cathedral and through all the windows with broken glass.

While the others were fast asleep in the cathedral – seemingly unimpressed by the terrible noise of the night – Lucia and Cordh sat worn out on a rickety bench in front of the portal at the west end, which was set back from the facade in ever diminishing, smaller arches. The large door was firmly jammed in and couldn't be budged by a millimetre. The hinges and lock had rusted away, but the wood itself was in relatively good condition. Even though only a few drops of rain could reach them here, the damp cold weather still got into their clothes and made them shiver.

Cordh hadn't been able to get a wink of sleep and so had decided to stick his nose outside the cathedral for a minute. After he had got up, he had spotted Lucia lit up briefly by a flash of lightening as she sat on the wall and looked out to sea. She was shocked when he suddenly appeared next to her. With an overexaggerated jerk of his head, Cordh suggested they went outside together so they could chat without waking the others, as they would otherwise have to shout to be heard over the roar of the storm. Lucia agreed with a nod and they both headed off along the outside wall to the portal where the bench was standing.

"Xenos has no idea about what's going on," said Lucia loudly, "but he does seem to know how to survive. His memory only starts from when he arrived in the city, but he must have managed to get here somehow." She looked over to Cordh on her right, who she couldn't actually see at this moment. "It is strange that he doesn't remember anything about his childhood. I've only ever heard about some memory loss affecting a certain period of your memory. But it is his whole life ... I am really not sure what to think."

Cordh nodded in the dark. "Do you think he's dangerous?"

"If only we knew. Probably no more than any of us, to be honest, although his loss of memory does raise a lot of questions. What actually triggered it? Was it the incident which left him with that scar on the back of his head? If so, why doesn't his memory go back further and end at the point when he got the injury?"

"Or he's playing tricks on us, like Sydell thinks," Cordh added.

"Who knows. But personally, I think something would already have happened by now if he had wanted it to. He knows how and where we live, he knows that he can get enough to eat here and that he can get it all by himself if necessary. He is not dependent on us at all."

"We just have to trust that he is not lying and that he'll tell us as soon as he remembers."

Lucia leant forwards and stretched her hands. "I must admit though, I have a feeling that the community stops us being so careful. All of us know how hard life can be and we were all accepted into the group without any questions being asked. That is what I experienced anyway. That is not meant in a negative way either, I did become part of the group after all. But somehow I have the impression that we quickly forget or suppress the downside of all this whether you want to or not. Maybe because we all get on so well with each other and there seems to be no reason to worry too much about negative things."

Cordh leant back and felt the damp wood of the bench at his back. "That's certainly true. But what can you do? Driving someone away could lead to our first conflict. And there's nobody here that you wouldn't trust in the dark. You have to admit that. Maybe it would be different if something bad had happened. And like you said: if Xenos had been planning something, he would have done it ages ago already. However, I have to agree with what you say about getting careless. We ought to discuss that with the others. When he's not there."

Lucia nodded and closed her eyes. She took a deep breath of fresh air which made her feel slightly light-headed.

They sat there on the bench a bit longer without saying a word, while the storm turned to head further inland and slowly but surely disappeared, as did the ever-weakening rain.

By the time dusk had set in, Lucia was alone. Cordh had said his goodbyes a little earlier to try and get some sleep, which had obviously worked as he hadn't returned. She, however, had lain down on the bench and watched as the heavens got lighter and lighter, revealing the clouds torn asunder by the storm, which was soon lit up by the golden light of the morning sun. At some point her eyes closed and she fell asleep.

Chapter 16

Escalation

Early afternoon, a slight tug on her shoulder stirred Lucia from her sleep. It was Beauford.

"Good morning, or is that good afternoon," she rasped, smiling slightly and gently rubbing the sleep out of her eyes.

"I'm not so sure about that," he said and took a step back.

She straightened up, immediately feeling the price in her bones for the hours spent on the unyielding bench. "Why? What's up?"

"You need to come with me first," he said. Waiting until she got up and stretched, he led her down to the passageway on the north side of the west wall.

At the corner, Lucia could already hear voices from inside the cathedral without being able to discern what the commotion was about.

Bemused, she stopped as she stepped into the cool shadows of the masonry. When they looked up and saw her, it suddenly went quiet.

Close to the extinguished campfire stood Cordh, Xenos and Forg.

Sydell was crouching next to where she had been sleeping, hastily gathering up her belongings. Despite all this activity, she was still holding onto her combat knife, eyes fixed on the others. Seeing Lucia, she paused momentarily, her chest rising and falling heavily. Adrenalin had sharpened the woman's senses.

"What's going on here?" demanded Lucia, unable to make sense of it all. All eyes were fixed on her.

She took in Xenos, standing there barefoot and barechested. His right hand covered an apparent wound on his upper left arm – blood had left a trail down the back of his hand, across his wrist to the middle of his little finger, from where it was dripping onto the floor. Some blood had also made it between the fingers of his right hand. The wound wasn't bleeding very much with only an occasional drop dripping to the ground to be soaked up by the dust; it probably looked worse than it actually was.

All eyes turned back to Sydell, who was packing more things into her backpack.

Lucia felt like a detective, attempting to collect information on the trail of a crime. Or like one of those games she liked to play with her parents where someone describes a scene – a strange accident or an apparent murder – and the others have to find out what happened by asking simple questions requiring "yes" and "no" answers. As long as you kept getting "yes" answers you could carry on asking. If the answer was "no", the next in line took over.

"I was having a wash behind the cathedral in the upper cabin," explained Xenos, "and I didn't have a towel with me. So, I put on my trousers, tucked the rest of my clothes under my arm to get out of the way because I knew Sydell was waiting outside. Cordh was sitting a bit further away in the grass. He'd said he would let Sydell go first. I'd heard that. Just when I was passing her, she suddenly pulled out her knife and came at me."

"I was just able to keep her off him, otherwise she would have stabbed him," Cordh added, the horror still clearly written in his face.

"Why don't you show everyone your tattoo," blasted Sydell, turning to Xenos and pointing at him with the knife.

Xenos raised his left arm. Below his armpit was a dark blue hash sign and under this a narrow, vertical, long bar; a smaller hash sign below that. Left and right of the upper end of the bar were two parallel horizontal bars with the upper bars slightly longer than the lower ones.

Everyone took a look at the tattoo.

Sydell spoke again: "This is the *Iron Dragonfly*. No surprise if it doesn't look familiar to you: in most cases no one who sees it survives to tell the tale. And that is precisely why we've got just two options here: either this guy's playing games with us or he's a *scout*. Why? If he's not a *scout*, he must be playing a lying game. Anyway, this tattoo makes him a *hunter*, with or without a weapon. And even if he did lose his memory, it doesn't change the fact that we've all been in danger since he got here, even if there has been nothing to show for it so far." She looked deep into Xenos' eyes. "What are you doing here?"

Xenos, who had taken another look at the tattoo, raised his head and gave Sydell a baffled look. He seemed to know that she would not believe him, no matter how he answered.

Lucia remembered that Xenos had washed and dressed in the cabin shortly after he had arrived. It had probably just been a coincidence that nobody had noticed the tattoo before. Lucky perhaps for Xenos. At least it showed her that Sydell's threat the other day was not an empty one.

"I don't understand," admitted Lucia, not alone with the thought. "What is the *Iron Dragonfly* and how come you know that hardly anyone survives to tell the tale later?"

Sydell, still trying to get her things into her backpack, looked up. She had to admit that she was not going to get everything in by being so hectic and disorderly. "Originally, the *Iron Dragonfly* was a tightly organised guild with clear objectives, but for ages now the bulk of them have been a loose band of murderers, lunatics and perverts all up to no good under the fellowship of this sign. However, there is a bunch of I don't know how many members and groups still loyal to the old values. The dividing line between the two gets blurred now and again. In the end, it doesn't matter why you die or who kills you."

She spoke quickly. It was clear she was keen to get going.

Still, she went on: "A few years ago, I came across a small town where a group of people had been wiped out. Well almost: one poor guy was still alive and told me about the attack. That's when I first heard about the *Iron Dragonfly*. Stories are also passed around in whispers, but you don't peddle them. You never know if there is a *scout* around listening in.

"So, having heard the story of the *Iron Dragonfly*, the guy urged me to steer clear of any confrontation and to cut and run at the slightest sign." She looked around at everyone for a moment. "And I'd advise you *to do the same.*"

"What happened to the man?" asked Lucia.

"He died from his injuries the following night."

"Any of you ever heard of this?" Cordh asked the group.

"Only what Sydell just told me," explained Beauford, giving the impression that he was uncomfortable talking about it, "that there are two kinds of *Iron Dragonfly* disciples: the old guard and those who are practically sailing under foreign flags. They say that any encounter is basically a death sentence."

"That word 'flag' is a pretty good word, by the way," threw in Sydell. "You know that the tattoo is a war flag."

Beauford went on: "And they say that no one would ever use the sign recklessly. In the end you never know who will see it, because not every member of the *Iron Dragonfly* actually wears it. So you never know who is part of it and who isn't. I don't know any more. I don't even remember where I picked that up."

"And so what's this all about?" Forg wanted to know.

"I should get the hell out of here and not be bothered with stories," Sydell said, looking around in all directions. "That's probably the best thing to do, I've got no desire to get killed by that one" – she pointed at Xenos again with the knife – "or anyone who might be following on because he's here."

No one responded; but everyone knew that from now on a shadow would lie over the peace and freedom they had found in this city.

Chapter 17

Persistence

"Would you mind telling me what you know?" asked Lucia, who was now completely alone with Sydell in the cathedral.

"There's not enough time for that," she said, without looking up. She had put her combat knife down for a moment so she could pack her things more easily.

"But it would be a big help for us," explained Lucia. She knew that this was the moment when the group would just fall apart, in the same way it had come together over the last few months – by coincidence.

The men were clear on the fact that Xenos should not just be chased away or left behind. For Sydell though, it was unthinkable for her to stay with the group under such circumstances, even if that meant saying farewell to the people she had got so used to. And Lucia was somewhere in the middle between these two standpoints.

Sydell shook her head. "It's only helpful to know about the *hunters* and *scouts*, everything else is not so important. You won't even recognise them for what they are at first glance. If you could, then I would have left much sooner." She glanced fleetingly at Lucia: "Being distrustful and careful help a lot more than an old story. And I can't and don't want to stay here a moment longer."

"I would like to hear the story anyway." Lucia thought about it for a minute. "If things were so dangerous round here, we would surely have noticed it by now. Xenos has been with us for fifteen days already. And he was always near us. He couldn't have told anybody about us. So it is certain that nobody knows he is here with us."

"That is precisely the problem: you just can't know. What if he had crept outside at night unnoticed and reported to someone somewhere? What if he left info about us somewhere and is just part of an advanced party? What if the first *hunters* suddenly appear? What if people have been watching us secretly for weeks?

"Why would anyone do that?"

"To see if anyone else is part of our group and just isn't here at the moment, so they can kill more people all at one go. I don't know either. But what if that's true? That is all just a bit too much for me – too many incalculable risks." She picked up her knife, stood up and looked about her.

"Maybe the story will die with you ..."

Sydell pretended to laugh. "As if that would change the way the world is going, if it wasn't like that ..." She found the leather water bag she had sewn herself. It could be closed tightly with a wooden cork. This good piece of craftsmanship was hard to see in the half-light of the cathedral, made darker still by the murky glass in the windows. The odd ray of sun did make it through some damaged windows and the occasional hole in the roof, which lent the huge room a very peculiar atmosphere. "It is as irrelevant as the pictures, books and other cultural artefacts there used to be, as unimportant as what remains of the legacy which has already almost completely faded away. In the meantime, practically everything has returned to dust or is buried under the ruins and rambling plants."

She shoved the knife back into the sheath attached to her belt and checked the straps on her water bag. "What does it matter if a story dies with me or not? And I assume I am not the only person or even the last one to know it anyway."

"And just like you said before: 'you just can't know'."

Sydell sighed with a brief smile. She realised that Lucia was not going to give up so easily. On the other hand, since making her discovery she had the strong urge to leave this part of her journey behind her as fast as possible. If she knew about this city and Lucia had found out about it, it was absolutely possible – or even unavoidable – that the *Iron Dragonfly* knew about it as well: maybe a horde of them was entering the ruins of the city this very minute.

Lucia watched as Sydell closed and tied up her backpack. Silently she waited for a reaction.

III. Interlude

The Road

The whole area was shrouded in silence. The sun rose bit by bit forcing out the fog that had covered everything in the night. The clear blue sky appeared, then the first treetops, swiftly followed by bushes, shrubs and tall grasses. The more the fog disappeared, the more everything sparkled, wetted by the cool morning dew.

At some point the fog had disappeared completely and one could see the road, and its broken asphalt which had survived the decades. The lack of vegetation, with just a few clumps of grass and the odd shrub and thistles, meant it was easy to spot among the nearby meadows and woods.

Under the grass and the splendour of the many-coloured flowers, another colour appeared – the colour of blood. The ripped open bodies of women and men of all ages, and uncountable children. All of them stabbed and beaten to death. They lay there, partly on top of each other, some on their own or even with their arms and legs chopped off as if they had all just been thrown away like rubbish. The evil which had been down on this road left nature cold; some birds were still flying high up above the expanse of green, and others continued their singing from everywhere; insects buzzed around and the day was alive, as if nothing had happened ...

Chapter 18

First Waves

"It all started 130, maybe 135 years ago, as far as I know," Sydell explained, filling her water bag at the spring behind the cathedral.

Lucia stood by, watching as Sydell pressed air out of the leather bag to better take on water. On her shoulders she carried her backpack, which she had hurriedly filled with her most important belongings as well as provisions to keep her going for a few days – everything else she'd left behind in the cathedral.

They had both agreed that Lucia could accompany Sydell part of the way to hear the story – at least the episodes that Sydell could remember. After that, they would go their separate ways: Lucia planned to return to the city with the new knowledge she had gained, while Sydell would go off alone and fend for herself again.

The others had set out for the harbour to fish, knowing that any discussion with Sydell was pointless and that she could not be dissuaded to drop her plan. They were somewhat surprised by Lucia's decision, but she had stood firm. As Sydell was keen to get going, Lucia's decision had to be made hastily. Sydell wanted to leave, alone or not.

Lucia knew that she would regret it forever if she didn't take this last chance. She knew there was no going back for Sydell; the story would go with her and disappear somewhere.

Concerned, Beauford had wanted to know what would happen next. Lucia had assured him that she would soon be back in the city to share the new knowledge and keep it alive. Afterwards they had said their goodbyes, with Xenos waiting a little to one side so as not to provoke Sydell. The fact that everything had happened so suddenly affected everyone in the group, especially since in the few last weeks and months the group had grown ever closer and everyone was seen as a vital part of the community.

"All over the world the mood had been tense for years. On the one hand you had the poor people and on the other hand the rich guys, a famine here and a war there – all for the sake of power, land and raw materials. They didn't just fight with weapons, but with lies too. Politically, it was just a mess. Things were decided that went completely against common sense. Other decisions restricted people's personal freedoms and paternalism was the be all and end all, even though all the talk was about democracy. There were those who ruled and had something to say, and those who were ruled and never had a choice. Of course, there were rebellions, some even succeeded and brought about change, but most people were like sheep, accepting everything; most people around the world were either too damned lazy and or cowardly to join forces and make a difference. Riots were put down with much bloodshed. Some just stifled. Of course, everyone was getting really distressed by it all, but hardly anyone did anything or even thought about doing anything for fear of the consequences."

Sydell stood up, pressing the wooden cap into the opening of the water bag.

"This increasing disenfranchisement also affected things you just couldn't run away from. Even something as bizarre and stupid as the packaging of food. Garbage was becoming a huge problem and there was nothing that any one individual could do about it. Hardly anyone was in a position to be completely self-sufficient and to live isolated from the rest of the world so as not to be a part of this manic machine that was destroying the environment for profit. And since politics and economics were brothers in arms, I mean you could say that the web of oppression was just squeezing the life out of people all around the world.

"These problems gradually caused people to commit suicide – I mean, they were literally doing it in public, too. On the one hand, they were protesting against the conditions, on the other hand I suppose they were just trying to find peace with nature. I guess they didn't want to have anything more to do with the whole system and suicide was their only option."

Sydell walked towards her backpack lying in the grass next to the spring and sat down on it, laying the water bag on the ground.

Lucia frowned. "Suicide as a kind of protest?"

"Yes. That caused more of a stir than any demonstration.

"All in all, things were already bubbling up, and it was just a matter of time before the whole catastrophe over-flowed the world. Times were moving towards revolt. But there was a difference. Some people wanted change because they themselves were being trodden on. Closer collabo-ration between countries upset economic foundations and excessive immigration threatened identity; politicians were just doing what they wanted. Others, on the other hand, didn't trust the media and all this fake news. They didn't believe all this, instead they looked around with their own eyes and with their own unclouded view of the world. Even then, you didn't need to know everything about the world to realise what was going on and to make up your own mind. Just like we do today and as it may have always been. I suppose you have to be an expert to understand what's going on in space, but most people know the difference between right and wrong without being an expert in any particular field. You just need to look and think. Over half the population of the world at that time was wiped out, killed through senseless information that diluted or falsified the facts, or just completely hid the truth."

"When I hear it that way, I can understand that some people just wanted to escape," Lucia reflected.

Sydell checked the lacing of her boots and nodded. "There were people who set themselves on fire in public, others suddenly stopped on highway bridges, got out of their vehicles and jumped to their death. At that time, the rising rebels were not attacking bystanders, as had been the case time and again either for religious or tactical reasons. As I said, it all started at about that time and took a while until this new consciousness gathered pace with people not wanting to accept the conditions under which they were supposedly living a free life. Ideas spread and were turned into action. Don't forget though that all this was happening in well-off, developed countries; I mean, there were always countries and areas around the globe where war, hunger and oppression were the order of the day and where these poor people had no chance to change their situation anyway."

She stood up and carefully packed away the water bag in a side pocket on her backpack. "At the beginning, not many people took their own lives like that. Maybe 50 or so among the billions worldwide. Of course, many more were thinking about it, as if admiring the consequence of those who killed themselves, but they didn't actually find their own lives bad or constricted enough to top themselves voluntarily. For many, having a family and a nice house were more important than freedom."

Chapter 19

A Vicious Circle

Something was missing.

He had a job and earned his livelihood, he had friends and acquaintances, a nice apartment and enough opportunities to fill up his spare time. He hadn't been in a relationship for a while, but that didn't bother him; physical desire was just a drive and he had no long-term plans to pass on his genes to the next generation anyway – especially not in these times.

Objectively, he was doing fine. And yet something was missing.

There were days when he felt good: floating along, life sorted out. On other days he would not venture out – unless he had to. He would sit around apathetically, start this and that but quickly lose interest. Or he would sleep most of the time. He would shut himself off completely, letting the hours and days go by without achieving anything. And then again there were moments when he felt a fire burning inside that he could not control; he felt that he had to leave, but where would he go? Weighing up the possibilities, he would just stand still until the fire had consumed everything except the inert, empty shell.

But what was the point? Existing. Wasn't he incarcerating himself, if he left everything the way it was? Wasn't he just wasting his life, if he failed to break through the walls of this imprisonment and set out on a *New Path*?

For months now, his thoughts had been circling around the same theme over and over again. Some things had been occupying him for years, but now everything seemed to be coming together, forming a single picture that was gradually standing out from the restlessly wafting mist of his mind.

In the end, what remained was the realisation that he had only this one life. When he compared himself with all the deadbeats out there, he saw that change was actually an option and that he could possibly create something of permanence. It was just a matter of security. Was he willing to give up all that he had worked for and been lucky enough to gain? Was he ready to start all over again?

The longer he pondered over these thoughts, the clearer his ideas and the more courageous his blazing heart became ...

Chapter 20

Birth of a New Sun

"It would be possible to change things, you know," said the driver. He was in his early twenties and for the last three years he had been keeping his head above water with a variety of odd jobs so as to have time to work out what he expected from life, and what he should be aiming for.

The car was parked on a car park which ran parallel to the beach. Its slightly raised position meant it was the perfect place to watch the sunrise from – which was due any minute.

"And how's that going to work?" his passenger asked, taking a swig from the wine bottle before handing it back to him. He was also in his early twenties, studying mechanical engineering and fully financed by his parents. They believed he should focus on his studies rather than on distracting jobs or having to think about where he should get enough money from for food and rent; they had no idea that he preferred living it up or that he spent the majority of his monthly allowance on weed.

"For example, if everyone who didn't normally vote actually did, and then they all voted for the same party," was his reply. "It wouldn't even have to be a party with a particular plan. It would simply be about showing the ruling class that they shouldn't feel too certain of their own position, even if they have sadly been sure of it for decades."

"That'll never happen," said the passenger and looked over to his left where he could see a man jogging along the beach with his dog running along beside him constantly looking up at its master.

"Exactly," agreed the driver as he glanced in his rear-view mirror, "because somehow everyone still seems to be satisfied, even if this opinion is based on the fact that somewhere someone else is starving, while your fridge at home is still half full." He took a swig from the bottle. "People are still not doing badly enough."

The passenger was still watching the man on the beach.

They could hear the gentle sound of the waves washing over the sand, and from somewhere behind them the first birds had started up their chorus in the trees accompanied by the sound of wailing sirens wafting over from the city. The air was pleasantly cool and the fresh smell coming in through the fully wound-down window announced that it was going to be a hot day. Up above threads of clouds drifted across the sky and the strip of light on the horizon grew brighter and brighter.

"And we can expect nothing," said the passenger. "And who from anyway?"

The driver nodded. "Elections would certainly be one way of doing it. But there is another way."

His passenger stopped watching the jogger, who had long since passed them following the line of the beach off to the right.

"There is one important question here. Would people be prepared to give everything up and commit their lives to a vision? I've been thinking about this for a long time."

"Have you found a solution yet?" the passenger asked.

The driver nodded, took a swig and handed the bottle back.

"And what is it?" asked the passenger before taking another mouthful of wine.

In front of them the first reddish edge of the blazing sun appeared over the horizon, instantly changing the light and the mood, while the man on the beach disappeared into the distance with his dog.

The driver was watching how the sunlight tinged the clouds with colour and gave his brief answer: "I am going to drop everything – and change the world."

Chapter 21

Conglomerate

"And that's how it all began?" asked Lucia.

The two women had been marching inland towards the east for some time.

"More or less," said Sydell. "I don't want to repeat myself, but it was a long process that began with this idea. Little by little, plans were formed that became more and more concrete as more people joined in. A network was created that only those who were involved knew about. There were people of all sorts, from students and workers to lawyers and company bosses. Secrecy was important because you couldn't risk anything being exposed. Later even members working for the police and secret services joined.

"There were also a lot of dropouts in the network who joined the cause because they had no other prospects or meaning in their lives. Political activists and conservationists also jumped on the band wagon as well as racists and social Darwinists. It didn't take long for way-out, esoteric groups to make their entrance. Some believed that the continents had their own consciousness and that they, the continents, ensured that wars were fought so they could actively participate in shaping the world. Or they interpreted the existence of the network as preparation for an upcoming event that depended on planetary constellations."

"Wasn't there any conflict between so many diverse groups?" asked Lucia, who was overwhelmed by the story, and particularly fascinated by the concept of continents having their own consciousness.

"Not at first, because everyone pulled together. It had also become an unwritten law that you could neither leave the network nor tell outsiders about it. Whoever broke this law was eliminated. Just like the outsiders who had learned about the network. This also applied to all of the members of the network's families. Everyone monitored everyone else and indiscretions were not tolerated, no matter who committed them.

"Those who threw themselves heart and soul in the network gave up their dreams and wishes. They knew that every life was replaceable and that sometimes they had to sacrifice their own desires if they wanted to pursue the goal of the network. Unconditional surrender of the self was also an indicator of the purity of conviction that stood behind everything and that was essential. Many were not up to this, which caused the ranks to thin out again and again. That's why they had to constantly ensure that one rotten apple didn't spoil the others."

"And what was the goal?"

"In the beginning, the plan was to instigate a nationwide rebellion in order to break the existing balance of power. The idea spread quite quickly, so that soon it was no longer about one country, but about a worldwide project. The aim was to seize power from the banks and large corporations as well as from misguided politicians. But over time things changed.

"The momentum within the network created an energy that drove everything forward to achieve the idea of movement and change. On the one hand, there was self-surrender, with no fame or glory attached, and on the other hand, the followers increasingly freed themselves inwardly from the constraints of society, taking care to remain inconspicuous to the outside world in order to protect the network. This meant that a loving family man, who earned his money in an office as a tax consultant, didn't spend his free time in his garage tinkering with his grandfather's vintage car, but instead was holed up in a basement with computer freaks simulating various scenarios, such as how to make entire financial systems collapse as skilfully as possible.

"Ultimately, it all culminated in the plan to make the world as we knew it collapse completely to create a *New World Order*. Up to this point everything had been just vague theory in the fantasies of the members, a war on many fronts, sometimes with more and sometimes with less victims and success. Now there was a fixed goal, and all efforts were concentrated on this."

"The *meltdown* 98 years ago..." said Lucia.

Sydell nodded. "Everything was leading up to this day. During the years of preparation, members of the network systematically penetrated the highest levels of government and all corporations that had a significant influence on important processes in the modern world. For example, oil companies, the arms industry and the military, or electricity companies. Or they founded small groups that could strike with their special knowledge – nothing was to be left to chance and everyone was eager to do his or her part so that the world would never forget that day."

Lucia looked back briefly. The cathedral had long since disappeared behind the trees of the dense forest they were walking through. On her way back, she would only have to keep westward, and then follow the coast, if she wasn't able to reach the city directly. She wasn't worried, but nevertheless, she would try to memorise rough landmarks in the landscape here and there.

"Everything went according to plan. The result was the worldwide destruction of energy supplies, infrastructure and the economy. The complete collapse of modern civilisation.

"In the course of those plans, the symbol of the *Iron Dragonfly*, which Xenos wears, was also created."

"Why a dragonfly?" asked Lucia.

"The man who told me all of this couldn't say. I think it's because the dragonfly has sharp eyesight and is a master of flight. If you think about it, the upper echelons of the network had their sights on everything, even if the whole system was supposedly split and became more and more autonomous towards the lower levels. But without a central authority that held the invisible threads together, a goal like that would never have been achieved, precisely because of the number of participants and their different views and motivations. The dragonfly's flying skills is probably another reason, because at that time, the whole world could be infiltrated silently, quickly and without error. Perhaps this creature was also chosen because it is beautiful and yet a robber." Sydell shrugged her shoulders slightly.

"I'm just surprised that something like this really worked and could be planned and kept secret for over three decades."

"It can only have been a matter of discipline. During the attacks, they even made sure that buildings and companies were also targeted that were completely in the hands of the *Iron Dragonfly*, regardless of whether they had been taken over at some point or founded by members. This was intended to make any pending investigations more difficult. When one particular huge office complex exploded, even the man whose idea had started it all died. The exact circumstances surrounding his death could never be clarified. However, it is assumed that it was his intention to die on that very day.

"It is also interesting that he always held the highest rank within the *Iron Dragonfly*, regardless of the ideological development in all those years, which made him more of a spiritual father. For everyone he was *The hidden God*, as very few people within the network knew his whereabouts or identity."

Lucia silently wondered if the office complex Sydell was referring to, was the one Beauford had reported on: *The Tower*. Perhaps it had been the headquarters of *The hidden God*.

"The culmination of worldwide destruction was supposed to have been the end of the plan, the fulfilment of the vision. But it was not the end. Somehow it was only the beginning, because suddenly *hunters* and *scouts* appeared everywhere, who continued to systematically target the survivors, because it was assumed that it could go back to the way it was before, if mankind recovered; theoretically, it would only have taken a few people. If they had started to rebuild in a structured way, this would probably have motivated other people to help as well. So, the new goal was the complete extinction of our species. And if necessary, they would kill their comrades and then themselves since there was nothing higher and more desirable than this last plan.

"When the perfectly organised network disappeared, this led to more and more battles and entire wars for power, resources and wealth. Religion and racism also became the basis for bloody conflicts again. Soon a new world war broke out, with everyone fighting against everyone else and with every means at their disposal, including chemical and nuclear weapons, which simply wiped out whole regions. It just turned into a mess that nobody could control. In the end the *Iron Dragonfly* proved to be the most resilient and won out, as the last power standing that could shape the world. I think its founder never expected things to turn out this way in his lifetime."

"I heard that the *Network* that was built up after the *meltdown* was destroyed and didn't only perish because the fuel for the generators ran out, among other things."

Sydell nodded and stopped. "That's true. It just meant that the downfall continued and speeded up, in fact. Because suddenly it wasn't even possible to transmit informations quickly over long distances anymore, so you couldn't find out about the conditions in other areas and other countries. People were finally isolated, because the *Network* of radio stations had up to that point still maintained the feeling of an undefined community. Despite the lack of reports from the airwaves, the disappearance of the *Network* also had a very demoralising effect, with the chance of rebuilding anything becoming even more remote."

Lucia, who had stopped at the same time, looked around.

They were standing on a hill with a meadow stretched out in front of them. Beyond that there was a sparsely planted birch forest, which disappeared into the distance to the left and right.

"But to come back to how it all could have turned out: the whole plan almost failed," continued Sydell.

"Why?"

"There was supposedly an informer who had found out about the attack on the office complex where the founder of the *Iron Dragonfly* had a company headquarters," Sydell explained. "If this attack and his death had been prevented, the plans would probably have been discovered. But before the informer could pass on his knowledge, he must have realised that the whole thing was far bigger than initially assumed. Or he realised that it was too late to stop everything."

This part of the story really reminded Lucia of her great-great-grandmother's experience. Could this also be a coincidence? A coincidence, like the people with their stories meeting each other in the city? Every story was a part of this network.

"So, this is the past that formed everything as we see it now," said Lucia as they started walking again.

"Yes. I think many people knew that something was happening somewhere, they had a feeling. But at the same time, I think when it came to the *meltdown,* they were all equally surprised and shocked when they looked at what happened around them on *Day Zero.*

Soon they were in the midst of the dappled birch forest. All around them the light-coloured trunks rose from a carpet of moss, lush grass and fern, and above their heads a shimmering sea of leaves was rustling gently in the breeze. In some places brightly coloured flowers had managed to stretch their heads towards the sun, making this peaceful place even more beautiful.

The forest was somehow hypnotic, and they walked straight on, looking around in silence.

Chapter 22

The Silence of Decay

"What's going to happen next?" asked Lucia.

They now found themselves nearing the edge of the birch forest – it had been a lot larger than they had initially thought – where more and more oaks, beech and other deciduous trees were appearing amongst the birch. They were sitting in a decaying hall which was almost unrecognisable as the architecture had begun to disintegrate into the surrounding nature.

The floor and walls were almost completely covered with moss, while only one or two beams were left where the roof had been, almost floating over the two women like the remains of a skeleton. Here and there creepers were hanging down into the hall, waving slightly in the breeze which was so gentle you could hardly feel it on your skin. The rest of the roof had collapsed into the hall where the floor had sunk down over the decades and was now filled with water so clear and smooth that it created the most amazing optical distortions and reflections. Apart from the odd bit of birdsong from a variety of birds which only just reached the women's ears, not a sound was to be heard; there was a real feeling of peace which made this place seem like part of a beautiful dream.

After Sydell had related her tale, Lucia told all the stories she had heard from the other members of the group as well. Sydell listened to these fragments gratefully, it was like slowly revealing the parts of an old stone tablet while carefully removing the earth it was covered in so that one could read the inscription all in one go; if Lucia had not come along with her, she would probably never have got to know all this.

"A good question," answered Sydell, who was sitting on her backpack glancing round the hall. "I will start relying on my gut feeling again and continue my march. Maybe more towards the south." She looked over to Lucia who was standing a few steps to the right in front of her leaning her forearms on a rusty bannister. She also looked around. "You wanted to go back, didn't you? Or have you changed your plans?"

The air in the hall was cool and smelt of dampness and moss. The shadows grew longer and the sky was slowly losing its bright blue colour, as the day prepared to give way to night.

"I am not really sure to be honest," admitted Lucia, without turning around to face Sydell. "On the one hand, I wonder if it's worth turning back. On the other hand, I don't know what lies ahead if I don't. I did tell the others I would come back to share the story. It would be unfair to disappear without a word because they would be worried otherwise. But in the end, it doesn't really matter."

"You can never be sure whether a decision like that is right or wrong, never mind whether you realise it immediately, much later or even never. In the past it would have been easier to work out, but nowadays other things count." She was watching Lucia. "Looks as though you are at a crossroads."

Lucia nodded. "I think so too."

IV. Interlude

Escape

He ran; and he heard voices calling to him.

He hastily fought his way through the tall grass and brushwood to get to the woods as fast as possible to find cover. It felt like everything was in slow motion, although all the sounds crowded in on him just as they normally would.

He held his hands up protectively in front of his face when he finally reached the edge of the wood and headed into the undergrowth. He realised that blood was stuck to him all over his skin and clothes. He suddenly paused and tried to notice whether he had been injured anywhere.

The back of his head hurt. He carefully felt what turned out to be a bleeding wound, although he couldn't say how he had got it. But that certainly wasn't the source of all the blood.

The voices were becoming even more animated, shouting threats after him. He couldn't understand everything, but he definitely knew that he had to get as far away as possible from his pursuers, and that he wouldn't survive if they found him – even if he had no idea what had happened or why he was fleeing.

He looked up from his blood-smeared arms and continued to run.

He had to get deep into the woods to make sure he had the chance to stop for a while and get his breath back so he could work out what to do next.

The calls from his pursuers slowly got quieter. But he knew they would never forget his face.

Chapter 23

Dance of the Lights

Sydell and Lucia were completely captivated by the sight before them: the hall was filled with a myriad of fireflies darting this way and that, their glowing numbers multiplied by the reflections on the water and the many surfaces in the hall. The two women were silent as they witnessed this magical moment. Lucia took a drag on her cigarette and passed it to Sydell. They were sitting on the floor not far from the door into the hall and leaning comfortably with their backs against the wall watching the spectacle.

Somewhere outside the hall crickets were chirping, while the full moon peeped in and out from behind passing clouds, intensifying the glow of the fireflies at one moment and bringing the shadows to life the next.

Sydell made the tip of the cigarette glow.

"Actually, it doesn't matter what I do," said Lucia, breaking the silence that seemed to have lasted for an eternity. "I can twist and turn it any way I want, it won't get me anywhere." There were two possibilities: go back to the city or stand alone. The third option, if she was honest with herself, was out of the question. They had never discussed it, yet she knew that Sydell would never let anyone around her influence her decision. Sydell was not like anyone else in the city; she was destined to go her own way without thinking of anyone else.

"You're right, but you can't let yourself off the hook quite that easily," said Sydell, as she took another quick puff and returned the cigarette. "Today nothing has any meaning anymore, that's true. Regardless of the *Iron Dragonfly's* activities, we've long since passed the point of recovery for humanity, we will simply become extinct. And it wouldn't make any difference to our lives either if everything was rebuilt, because this is all we have and we have to manage as best we can. There is nothing left for us to really strive for, no real goal that can be pursued and achieved with strength and willpower. At least that's how I see it. In the past you had to find your way, which usually consisted of working to make a living and having a family. What I want to say with all this is that the world doesn't care what you do, that's true, but that is precisely why this decision is so important because there are no other goals, and because it won't be easy to change your mind again afterwards, if at all.

"If you were shipwrecked at sea and you saw two islands in different directions and you couldn't judge which was nearer, you would still have to choose one of the islands to swim to. You could drown on the way to one island because it is too far and you wouldn't have enough strength to get there, but on the other hand you would definitely die if you didn't decide and try to reach one of them. But once you have chosen, you can't just turn around because you don't know how far the other island is. So, your chance of survival would decrease even more just by trying."

Lucia smiled. That was true, of course.

"I don't have a real plan either," continued Sydell. "If it weren't for Xenos, I wouldn't have left the city. But now ... I just want to wander around the world, see beautiful places and survive for a few years. You never know what tomorrow will bring."

"Yes," said Lucia and took another drag.

"Where does your gut feeling tell you to go?" asked Sydell.

Lucia tried to ignore all the consequences of the two possible decisions that she had gone over time and time again and tried to grab the first answer that whispered in her ear. "I would choose the city."

"Then you should do that."

"We may never meet again." Just saying these words made Lucia feel sad, as this thought would inevitably become a fact. If Sydell had suggested travelling together, with a heavy heart she would have had to say no; with every step she would have felt guilty towards Sydell – as well as towards herself, and the others.

"Not in this life," said Sydell, looking at Lucia, whose outline she could barely see now. "But I would be careful and would not go straight into the city. Observe the situation from a safe hiding place because you have to be prepared for everything."

Lucia nodded. "I don't like the idea at all. What if I get to the city and there's no one there anymore?" She didn't even want to think about the possibility that they were all dead.

"Then I would run like hell," was the short answer. "I can't and do not want to wait, especially not here, because standing still means weakness. You quickly become a target."

Lucia nodded again and took a drag. "I would probably think the same way if I were you."

"Life and experiences shape everyone. The fact that I'm a loner has upset a lot of people. But that's the way it is: Everyone has to be responsible for themselves and I would like to be solely responsible for my own death, if possible."

Lucia gave her the cigarette.

"But you shouldn't even think about it," continued Sydell. "Go back to the city. They will all be there and in good health. Just be careful of Xenos and don't let him out of your sight. The whole thing stinks to high heaven, I'm sure of it. With the tattoo on his body, he *is* a member of the *Iron Dragonfly*, because no one is born with one."

In the darkness, Lucia nodded and heard Sydell exhaling the cigarette smoke.

No sooner had they lost themselves in the magic of nature than the dance of the fireflies had come to an end. Inexorably, the floating stars faded, throwing the two women back into the reality of moonlight and intense darkness.

They sat there together talking for a while longer, as the sky cleared more and more. Eventually they set up the camp for the night and sank into a dreamless sleep by the light of the moon, which was now almost exactly above them ...

V. Interlude

At the Stream

After he had been walking and often running for the whole day and night without a break, he allowed himself a short rest at a small stream at the edge of a coniferous forest. He knelt down in the grass and held his hands, which were encrusted with dirt and blood, in the gently rippling water that sparkled in the sunshine. The feeling was instantly refreshing and cooling. He washed his hands, his arms, and then his face; the cold water was energising, even though he knew that he would soon have to find sleep to regain his strength.

Perhaps he could sleep in a cave or under an overhang, that would protect him from the weather, in case it got worse, but it would also hide him from searching eyes – even if he was pretty sure that no one had been on his tail for a long time. A hollow tree trunk would also do, as the branches and leaves would provide good camouflage.

While on the run, he had still not come any closer to finding out why he was in this situation at all. Everything was and remained a mystery. At least the wound at the back of his head had stopped bleeding.

After he had cleaned himself up and drunk plenty of water, he stood up and looked around listening intently. But he could neither see nor hear anything unusual. Hastily he took off his clothes and washed them in the stream to remove the worst of the blood and other dirt. In his haste, he only half-heartedly squeezed out his clothes before dressing again – the sun would dry everything quickly enough, and until then he wanted to enjoy the pleasant coolness on his skin.

He would have to decide which way to go next while he was on the move because the mere thought of staying in one place made him nervous. So, he spontaneously jumped over the stream and decided to keep going in the direction he had chosen. From now on, however, he only wanted to walk at a brisk pace and not run, so that he could conserve his strength and keep a careful eye out for food.

As he left the dense forest behind him, he crossed a lush meadow surrounded by forested hills gently sloping into a small hollow. Beyond that a new hill rose and behind it several rows of other hills; the scene reminded him of waves of algae in the water. He could make out numerous groves, and in the distance large areas of woods. Everything seemed to be in motion: Flowers and grasses waving in the breeze, while the shadows of clouds moved quickly over the land and the tops of the trees rustled in the wind.

Looking at the sky, the weather looked settled for the rest of the day. This calmed him down a bit, as he had no idea whether he would be able to find shelter for the night anywhere on the other side of the valley.

Chapter 24

Xenos

After Sydell had said goodbye to Lucia, she continued her way eastward, while Lucia went west to get back to the city. Both women's hearts had been heavy when they shook hands and embraced briefly as they parted. Their lives had imperceptibly converged in recent years and finally crossed in the city more than two months ago. From now on, they would move away from each other again and lose themselves in the vastness of the continent. The knowledge of this inevitability brought them both close to tears.

When alone, Lucia went at a very different pace to Sydell and made much slower progress, but that didn't matter much to her. Now she was able to reflect on her conversations with Sydell and think about herself.

Two days later, in the early evening, she reached the edge of the city – she had hit the coast a few kilometres further south and had been able to see the city in the distance from a high cliff. Following Sydell's advice, she moved carefully and vigilantly under the protection of the vegetation in an arc from the southeast towards the cathedral. She observed the city and the surrounding area for a few moments from several vantage points, so that she could detect any possible movements – which wasn't easy, as the the sun was blinding at times.

Furtively, she edged closer and closer, until she had a clear view through the undergrowth to the meadow on the east side of the cathedral, where the two cabins were located beside the source of the small stream. About 10 metres to her right, she could see the toilet hut in the shadows between the trees.

The area was quiet; she could only hear the singing of some birds and the sound of a light breeze through the treetops, as it gently touched her skin and carried the smell of the sea to her. At that moment she realised that this smell had been imperceptibly missing in the last few days.

In the cool shade of the cathedral, Lucia observed the gigantic structure. She held her breath for a moment, closing her eyes to concentrate on detecting voices or movements.

She opened her eyes, inhaled the fragrant air and wondered where everyone was. But before her thoughts could go any further, she heard something.

She recognised Forg, Beauford and Cordh running from the southern side of the cathedral and approaching the nearby forest.

"I'm back!" cried Lucia to draw attention to herself.

Forg stopped, while Beauford and Cordh continued to charge into the undergrowth. He looked to the left, thinking he had heard a voice.

"Forg!" cried Lucia and hurried towards him, protecting her face from the branches with her hands.

He recognised her and called out: "Come with me! And no questions!" With that he turned away and ran after the others.

Lucia turned sharply left and ran deeper into the woods again, trying to keep the others in sight, who had a lead that was not easy to catch up on – if at all. Panic spread through her. What if she couldn't keep up? Would she be completely on her own? What would happen next? Would the others wait for her or even look for her? And what had happened? What were they running away from?

As she followed the men, she wondered if the escape had anything to do with Xenos – she looked back and found to her relief that no one was on their tail.

Only then did she realise that each of the men was carrying his backpack. Were they finally leaving the city? And where was Xenos?

The ground continued to rise for a while before it started to fall off slightly. Meanwhile the dense vegetation hardly changed. Walking this fast, Lucia had to be constantly alert and careful not to trip over a root or twist her ankle on the uneven ground.

She had no idea how long they had been running together, dodging trees and being lashed by branches, as she couldn't duck fast enough or protect herself with her hands. Lucia's legs became heavier and heavier and her lungs began to hurt, while the backpack kept banging painfully against her lower back. Despite all the difficulties, she was still able to keep the others in sight and not lose them – although catching up was out of the question.

At some point they reached the edge of the forest and stopped to take a breather and discuss together how to continue. Finally Lucia was able to join them.

"If that wasn't luck, I don't know what was," said Forg to Lucia, out of breath. "If we had left earlier or if you had gotten there a little later, we would have missed each other."

Beauford and Cordh, who had only realised after a while that Lucia was there and on the run with them, were as happy as Forg.

Lucia, gasping for air and exhausted, could only nod. She stood bent forward supporting herself with her hands on her thighs.

Forg put down his backpack, took a few steps away from the group and looked around. They seemed to be alone, as he couldn't detect anything unusual. All of a sudden, he felt like he had been transported back to the time when he had been on the run with Cordh.

"Where is Xenos?" asked Lucia, glancing briefly at Beauford, who also dropped his backpack.

"He jumped off one of the bell-towers this afternoon," explained Beauford, whose face was red from the exertion.

Lucia was startled. She would have liked to straighten up, but her lungs hurt. "Why?"

"He said his memory had come back."

"We just buried him in the cemetery earlier," said Cordh, panting and wiping the sweat from his forehead. He put his backpack on the ground in front of him and opened it. As they had left in such a hurry, he wanted to see what he had in it.

"I don't really understand," said Lucia looking at the men.

"Ah, you are in luck again," said Forg, walking slowly back to the others. "Because we can fill you in," he said with a smile – trying to lighten the mood.

Chapter 25

The Burden of Memories

Beauford had called Forg and Cordh to come and join him after hearing sounds coming from the upper part of the cathedral and not being able to find Xenos anywhere. Together they climbed to the top of the stone steps in the southern tower of the westwork where they parted company to search for Xenos. Beauford chose the southern tower and Forg the northern one – he had to be careful as they knew part of the building below had been destroyed and it was unclear whether any unseen damage might catch them out up here. Cordh headed for the gallery.

It was Beauford who found Xenos. It turned out that he had climbed out of a window in the southern tower and was standing on a ledge looking out into the distance.

After Beauford had called out to the others once again, they all ran past the rusty bell frame and the opulently decorated bell, and through the room which was completely covered in green moss and grass – that lush green, which everyone was amazed to find up here, made everything seem unreal.

Nobody knew what to say. They stopped in their tracks a few metres away and stared at Xenos, who realised he was no longer alone but continued to gaze out over the city, the sea and the sky which was dotted with a few lonely clouds.

"I now know what happened," said Xenos. He didn't give the others a chance to get a word in and continued: "My memories started to come back to me bit by bit. It was as if I was travelling to the different stations of my past.

"Before I came here, I had been roaming aimlessly around the wilderness for what seemed like an eternity because I was fleeing from something. I did *belong* to the *Iron Dragonfly*, Sydell was right about that. I was born into their ideas, their plans and their whole campaign. And yes, I did travel around as part of a group and I am responsible for the deaths of uncountable people. Until recently I was a *scout* and was always very good at my job. After all, they had been training me since I was a child. Some of us became *scouts*, the others became *hunters*. There was also this woman in the group, who was a *scout* as well. We were in a relationship together. One day she told me we ought to leave everything behind us, sneak away secretly at night and find somewhere quiet to settle down on our own. I asked her why she had come up with that idea. She then revealed that she was pregnant – by me, which was a bit of a miracle considering how unusual that is nowadays.

"Two days later our *hunters* slaughtered a group of people which other *scouts* of ours had discovered. There were no survivors. The next morning, we noticed that there was an unusually large number of children among the corpses, as if this group had somehow been blessed with fertility by some superior power. This strengthened our secret resolve to carry out our plan to disappear as quickly as possible and to start a new life.

"One day, some way away from the others, we were just talking about when would be a suitable time to make our escape, when one of the *hunters* came over to us. He said that we were all on a suicide mission now as there were fewer and fewer groups left which did not belong to the *Iron Dragonfly*. That inevitably meant that we would have to start wiping out other like-minded groups so that we didn't become the next targets ourselves and to ensure that we could then have a quiet life, knowing that we were among the last people to survive and that with our own deaths we could bring the old vision closer to completion or even actually make it reality.

"He then said that we should begin by killing all the people who endangered the solidarity within our own group as that was the unwritten law from the past. He had hardly finished what he was saying when he pulled out a knife and stabbed my partner. He stabbed her repeatedly in her belly, in her breast and in her throat while she sank to the ground.

It all happened so quickly that I couldn't react at first. Then I instinctively drew my knife and rammed it into his face. I stabbed him again and again. Screaming, he dropped his weapon while I stabbed him in the eyes, through his cheek and smashed his teeth in with the blade. When he dropped to his knees, I slammed the knife down into the top of his skull and he finally fell twitching to the ground and died.

"All the noise had alarmed the others, so I fled. They threw stones after me and hit me several times. Stupidly I didn't take my knife with me. Somehow, I managed to get into the nearby woods and got further and further away without them catching up with me.

"I had managed to suppress all memory of this and of all the terrible things that I had done, when the same thing was done to me that I had been responsible for doing to others over all the years. Until that day I had never had to dirty my own hands with blood, but that did not mean my role within the *Iron Dragonfly* was any less evil. And as a child of the *Iron Dragonfly* I couldn't remember even the smallest part of my life, just general sorts of knowledge and nothing personal at all. Sydell's words really had me perplexed to begin with, but at the same time bit by bit they uncovered all the memories that my consciousness had buried. I had seen my tattoo of course, but I had no idea what it meant. I had hoped to find the answer to these questions myself. After Sydell had spoken openly about her lack of trust in me, I knew that it would have to remain my secret. Firstly, because of her, and secondly, because of all of you, as you would certainly have asked me why I hadn't spoken about it before. There was no way forward and no way back, until my carelessness behind the cathedral led to the incident with Sydell.

"And I can't even say whether *scouts* or *hunters* are on their way here at this very moment. The longer you survive, the less likely you are to be caught. That's how it is these days.

"I can't even give you any advice. Just keep your wits about you. And forgive me."

With that, he let himself fall forwards and plunged into the depths below.

The men were rooted to the spot, unable to say a word, only the wind could be heard whistling up the stairway in the tower. It took them a few minutes before they felt able to make their way down again, to bury the body of Xenos – or whatever he was really called, he took his real name to his grave – so he could at least rest in peace.

Chapter 26

A New Era

They had left the woods and trekked across a meadow beyond, bordered by a pine forest entirely devoid of undergrowth. Since the sparseness of the trees made them an easy target, they had no option but to keep moving until they were somewhere that offered more cover. And so they stopped only for short rests to conserve their energy. After all, who could say when they would find a suitable place to camp or whether they would spend the night on their feet?

At the edge of a small grassy clearing, they came to a stop. Each of them had made sure that all essentials – such as a change of shoes – were stashed in their backpacks. Since they always carried their most important belongings with them, their losses were limited to the odd item of clothing. On the other hand, they had hardly any food and water. But they would find a solution for this too; at least they were alive.

As the sun moved westwards, a clammy shade descended into the forest.

"We were standing in the cathedral after the burial and wondering what to do next," said Beauford, taking a drag from his cigarette and instinctively covering the glow with his hand even though it was not yet so dark that it might have given him away. "To be honest, we were all feeling pretty rattled after what Sydell had done, not to mention the story Xenos had told us. We agreed to wait for your return before discussing our next steps."

"But then something happened," said Lucia, with a vague sense of foreboding.

"You can say that again," interrupted Forg, taking a small sip of water from a plastic bottle that was almost empty. He hoped they would find water in the next few hours for he had a raging thirst and would have liked to drink the entire contents of the bottle. But reason prevented him from doing so.

"I was standing by the remains of the wall drinking water from a cup when it was knocked out of my hand and I heard wood splintering," said Beauford. "I dashed for cover behind the wall and saw a bullet hole in the cup and another one in the seat of a chair just a few metres away from me. The cup had flown right over towards the chair."

"Couldn't you see anyone?" asked Lucia.

"It was probably a sniper from one of the tower blocks in the north of the city," explained Forg.

"I didn't even hear the damn shot," said Beauford. "I reckon they must have used a silencer, or we'd have heard it across that distance. But who knows ...?"

"And what about you guys?" asked Lucia, looking over to Cordh and Forg. She recalled her conversation with Sydell before they had set off. Sydell had speculated whether the group was being watched. Was it a coincidence? Or had her constant distrust led her to become obsessed with danger?

"I was sitting on the bottom step of the north tower and Forg on one of the chairs," explained Cordh.

"On one of the safe ones, it would appear," added Forg.

Cordh continued: "The bullet gave me the shock of my life. I was about to play something on the guitar, but I quickly forgot that idea." At these words, he realised for the first time that he no longer had the instrument with him. Although it would have slowed him down, he had always enjoyed playing it since he had found it in the city.

Lucia nodded.

Beauford stretched. "Anyway, we stayed away from the opening after that, but we had to do something. Basically, we might as well have been blind because we had no idea where the shot had come from, nor how many people were out there. I rushed as fast as I could from the wall into the cathedral, where I was better hidden. The others ran in an arc through the shadows to get to their sleeping quarters. We stuffed everything we could grab into our backpacks and hastily fastened them up. Then we ran to one of the doors in the south aisle and fled, in the hope that someone wouldn't already be waiting outside with a bullet for each of us."

"It probably would have got you if you hadn't come with us right away," said Forg, looking at Lucia.

"And now we're sitting here," she said. "But what I ask myself is: How long had they been waiting in the tower block?"

Beauford took another drag. "It can't have been that long. They could have taken us all out at once while we were burying Xenos."

"It's also possible," remarked Cordh, "that they'd arrived at some point and chosen a tall building to scan the city for people at their leisure. It would have taken a while."

"But the cathedral stands out so much, it's the first place I'd have looked for signs of movement," said Lucia.

Beauford nodded. "Xenos came from the north. It's quite possible that the shooter was a member of the group Xenos came from. At least, that would make sense. It would be illogical if it turned out his memory loss had been a pretence the whole time."

"Why?" asked Forg.

"Because he told us his story before he died."

Lucia frowned. "And what if it was made up?"

Shrugging his shoulders, Beauford said: "That wouldn't make any sense either. Why would he have told us a pack of lies right before his suicide?"

There were many unanswered questions, and they would probably never find out the truth. What mattered now was that they had all survived unharmed; everything else was secondary. Each was fully aware they had had narrowly escaped death. They would have to take more care from now on. In hindsight they were horrified at their own recklessness. What the hell had possessed them to split up and go out exploring alone? They shuddered at the thought.

They rested a while before heaving their backpacks onto their shoulders and setting off into the advancing dusk on a trail that would lead them further southeast.

Lucia wondered whether Sydell might also be travelling in the same direction, that they might eventually arrive at the same destination. She knew that meeting again was more wishful thinking than probability, but the thought gave her comfort because it would mean that Sydell was safe.

Over the next few hours, as they made slow progress through the darkness – the half-moon in a cloudless sky was of limited help to them down below the treetops – Lucia shared with the others what she had learned from Sydell about the *Iron Dragonfly*; the men were intrigued.

From time to time, they would pause for a break, for everyone was exhausted and longed for food. But it was the intense thirst that made each one of them feel their strength slipping away with every step.

As day broke, they finally left the forest – which in the obscurity of night had gone over into deciduous woodland but still offered no more favourable opportunities for a longer break than had the pines – and came to a vast area on which corn was growing as if cultivated and over which motionless wisps of fog hung, while in the east the sky seemed to be on fire. It was only a question of time until the sun would pour its golden light over the new day.

Everyone silently wondered if anyone lived here somewhere or if this vegetation was a freak of nature.

Even if the air, the landscape and the first birdsong of dawn appeared to signal hope, something else appeared that made this peaceful imagery fade into the background: in the middle of this strange field, whose gifts they gratefully accepted and whose boundaries they could not even begin to make out, a veritable forest of reeds appeared, rising like a bulwark before them and averaging over four metres in height. After they had fought their way through the dense tangle of plants, they found themselves – exhilarated, with wet feet and only a few little cuts – at the edge of a vast lake from which a flock of ducks took flight ...

Chapter 27

Paths

Their random journey took them to remote places and across desolate landscapes, always in search of water, food, supplies and a safe enough shelter for the coming night. They took it in turns to keep watch.

As the days passed, everyone realised they once more had their own instincts to rely on, since caution – coupled with distrust – and their inner voice became constant companions that held a protective hand over the four travellers.

Lucia gradually began not only to make a mark in her diary for each day, but also to write down what she had experienced and, most importantly, to record the events that had begun with her arrival in the city. She considered this point as the beginning of a new and the end of an old, difficult period of her life. She did not know what she was writing for, she just had a vague urge to do it. Each of them was sure that the end was coming and that it was unstoppable. So, in theory, there was no point in writing anything down, since the chances of anyone ever reading it were vanishingly small; and yet every evening she took the time to open her diary in a quiet spot apart from the others and put a few words to paper.

She increasingly wondered what Sydell was doing right now and whether it might have been better if they had all fled together; then they would have been spared this separation. What's more, Sydell's experience would most certainly have proven an asset to them – and her humanity an enrichment for the whole group. But their time together belonged to the past now. What if Sydell had since turned back to the city? Lucia could not bear to even think about it.

The longer she dwelt on it, the clearer it became that she felt lost as a woman. Cordh, Forg and Beauford were kind and decent, no doubt about it, but they were men who couldn't understand many problems – which is why she never talked about such things. While she was thinking, she recalled her conversations with Sydell which regrettably had begun too late in the day. That was another thing she could not change anymore.

On their way they came by a wind-farm several square kilometres in size, whose turbines enveloped by plants rose into the air like trees, and from whose rotor blades lianas hung down into the depths, gently swaying in the breeze, while creaking and groaning sounds emanated from the structures and the gnarled vines. The ground was shrouded under an almost impenetrable blanket of various creepers and roots; only in isolated places had grasses and flowers found a breach.

The entire place would have seemed distinctly eerie had it not been for the countless birds that nested under the shelter of the vegetation. During the day, the noise level was tolerable, as most of them were busy searching for food, but towards evening their chirping and singing would increase to a deafening chaos which only diminished after sunset, later giving way to an agreeable silence for a while before nocturnal species took up their lonely song.

Another time, they spent the night at the site of several gigantic hangars; some of them must have been over a kilometre long and in some cases more than two kilometres wide. Inside and out, creepers, mosses, ferns and grasses predominated. Wherever daylight could penetrate – by and large where the roof had fallen in – colourful flowers and lush trees stood out from the tangled mass like an oasis. Planes and helicopters, abandoned decades earlier, had become one with this *New World*. Here and there, large hollows had formed and gradually filled up with water, providing a thriving habitat for new plants and animals. Water dripped sporadically from the steel joists overhead, glinting in the sunlight as it travelled downwards. Some of the hangars resembled roofed woodland; their original purpose as forgotten as their creators.

In spite of all the fascinating places they chanced upon, their thoughts always returned to the city and what they had left behind: a sense of permanence, a refuge, a home. Now they were involuntary nomads once more, growing more aware with every step of the fate they must ultimately face. The city in their memories was a golden place; with lush green vegetation, the sparkle of sunlight on the pure blue sea and delicate white clouds punctuating the sky.

They had never known anything but this world, yet each had lived their childhood in the soothing assumption of immortality. Of course, every one of them had eventually grasped how short life is, though exactly when this insight had crept into their minds, they could not say. Or had it simply appeared one morning many years ago?

Each member of the group felt as if they were weighed down not only by their backpacks but also by some un-named burden that grew more leaden with every thought, spreading like a tumour in the soul the longer they silently trudged. The knowledge that they were not being pursued failed to reassure them. Even nature's magical gifts of rich colours, shapes and textures could not alleviate the pain and the weariness that gradually smothered them. As the days and weeks passed, so grew in them a vague sense that they might indeed be the last humans on earth; nothing had any meaning anymore since their escape from the *Golden City* ...

Chapter 28

The Grey Badlands

The transformation had been subtle at first: a dead bush here, shrivelled grass and an inky puddle there. Until, at some point, the group could no longer ignore the bleak spectacle that unrolled before them. They paused as they took it in.

"Have you ever seen anything like this?" whispered Forg bewildered, setting down his backpack to take a sip from his water bottle.

"No." Beauford let his gaze drift over the scene.

Lucia looked apprehensively at Cordh, who could only shrug his shoulders.

An expanse of coarse grass grew in feeble clumps, twitching rigidly in the breeze. Behind them, the silhouette of an odd tree or bush stood out – but the forest from which they had emerged had now vanished in the hinterland – while to the left and right a desolate no-man's land faded into the greyness of the day. On the horizon, however, they could make out what looked like some kind of industrial complex.

"Maybe a military base," speculated Forg, stowing his bottle away again.

"Or factories and warehouses," suggested Cordh.

"Let's find out," said Beauford.

Lucia hesitated. "What if there are people there?"

Beauford glanced at her, noting tersely: "Then I guess we've already been discovered."

He was absolutely right; everyone was aware of that. Besides, it was too late to turn back or bypass the place.

The sombre clouds moving slowly across the sky appeared to loom downwards. There was a curious absence of raindrops released from the dark, shredded rags that now threatened to enclose them.

An oppressive aura hung over the reinforced concrete structures with their rusting tangles of steel and became more overbearing as they approached.

Having passed the first ruins it became apparent that this could not simply be one of those ordinary industrial complexes that used to spring up around the outskirts of cities; for one thing, the dimensions were of a different order altogether; for another, sparse vegetation grew everywhere from the concrete carcasses, which themselves had become discoloured and pock-marked by the elements, their partially exposed skeletons making this spot even more terrifying than it might have been on a sunny day. Besides grasses and scrub there was very little, only a few sickly birches; anything more substantial was nowhere to be seen. Windowpanes were either cracked or had become opaque through the years, so that they let only a fraction of the original light into the buildings. Their open doors and gates resembled gaping maws.

Everyone could hear their own footsteps and those of the others on the patches of asphalt that covered the ground. And then there was the wind, which from time to time produced an eerie drone or whistle as it blew through rusted pipes and empty corridors; the remains of a tarpaulin fluttered, a tin can rattled around and a chain clanked against a metal barrel, a terrible sound that seemed to come from all directions and which eventually faded away, echoing softly.

There was no birdsong or buzzing of insects, which underscored the harsh, cold hostility of the place and reinforced the travellers' sense of foreboding.

They roamed the streets for what felt like an eternity, past deserted halls haunted by the mournful song of the wind, past stacks of iron girders that had rusted into one another to form misshapen mounds, undiscernible one from the next. Atrophied steel constructions cowered alongside buildings that had withstood the elements. And they saw sinister, towering chimneys of inconceivable dimensions and smokestacks that could have swallowed entire tower blocks.

Walking at some distance behind the others, Beauford took it in slowly, watching, listening. He paused in the middle of a large intersection and glanced to his right. His eyes wandered down and across the ground before him, where a few blades of grass had forced their way through a crack in the asphalt.

Cordh, who had been keeping an eye on Beauford, called to the other two. "Wait!"

Lucia and Forg stopped and turned to face Cordh. Only now did they notice that Beauford had dropped behind.

"What is it?" asked Cordh and walked over to Beauford, who lifted his gaze and once more looked to his right.

"I know why nothing's growing here," he said in a flat voice and turned around for a moment. He looked in the direction from which they had come. It was too late to walk back, he was sure.

As Cordh came closer, he followed Beauford's stare until his eyes alighted on a sight that made him, too, stop in his tracks.

Now Lucia approached with Forg and squinted into the distance.

"Probably a power station that collapsed at some point," suggested Forg casually and turned to continue on his way.

"Or a nuclear meltdown," murmured Beauford, his eyes fixed on the greyish blue ruin. It now began to dawn on him that perhaps it was no coincidence that everyone he had encountered in the *Golden City* seemed to be educated, knowledgeable about the past and had a sound grasp of how things interconnect – he had also met plenty whose minds were so atrophied that they were unable even to communicate properly.

Forg paused. "You reckon?" He couldn't comment at this distance. He didn't really want to, either. This place gave him the creeps and he wanted to get the trek over with as quickly as possible.

"Here, or maybe somewhere else," Beauford clarified. "I've seen photographs with my own eyes. The shape of the cooling tower – if that's what it is, judging by what's left of it – looks familiar. Of course, I can't be sure, but looking around, it seems a fair guess. But it doesn't matter now whether I'm right or not ..."

"... because we've exposed ourselves to the radiation," surmised Lucia. She didn't know exactly what that meant, only that they might become ill and die. She shuddered at the thought and wondered if Sydell might have been here too.

Beauford nodded. He was aware from stories about places like this and from his own day-to-day observations that nature can reclaim any place, even highly radioactive and contaminated ones; but the stunted vegetation of the vast space they had just crossed, coupled with the eerie silence now surrounding them, made him suspect that there was something in the air that even the smallest and simplest of creatures instinctively avoided. Of course, he might be mistaken, and the reason could be simply that they were standing on 10-metre-thick concrete with no groundwater or other life-giving medium where nature might gain a foothold. On the other hand, no one could escape the suffocating feeling that came out of every corner and from every direction. An unnamed horror was closing in on them.

"All we can do now is try to get across as fast as we can," said Beauford. He had heard of other nuclear accidents where flora and fauna had recovered sooner than expected, as if nothing had even happened. But whatever had happened here, it must have been on a catastrophic scale, worse than anything he could imagine. He dared not even begin to think about it.

"How long does radioactivity stay harmful for?" asked Cordh, who had to admit to having no idea whatsoever about such things.

"Without having more information, I'd guess about 200,000 to 300,000 years," replied Beauford. "At least. But it could also be millions of years."

Lucia recalled Sydell's story, and how she had spoken of rival factions that had fought with nuclear weapons. It was hard to comprehend that humans could have wrought such havoc that the planet was now littered with contaminated regions, poisoned for eternity. Was radioactivity perhaps the reason for the death of Beauford's wife? Had she been to a place like this without realising? Is that why she unexpectedly died in her sleep?

The group continued its march. Each one of them felt as if they were enclosed in a place entirely separate from the outside world, with every noise – including their own footsteps – becoming quieter as they sank deeper and deeper into their thoughts, until they found themselves moving through a world of utter silence, a grey world devoid of sound, of life and of hope.

Vanishing

The journey through the badlands continued to reverberate in their minds for a long time. It was as if they had travelled into their own personal future from which they knew they could not escape. It would take a long time, but eventually tree roots would one day penetrate the surface and begin to recapture this relic, this grey desert. None of them would live to see it, however; by then, all of them would have long disappeared from the face of this ever changing planet.

While they remained in the southern regions, they mostly shunned contact with other individuals and groups, trusting only their instinct and each other. Their narrow escape from the *Golden City* had taught them that much.

The months and years passed, and Lucia continued to record their experiences in a growing collection of what could no longer be described strictly as diaries, since she often wrote about her memories from the time before she met the others. The pages acquired an increasingly biographical tone. She regretted immensely not having started earlier, instead of drawing a line for each day. But what was the point of regret?

When she began to see them more as a burden than as mementoes – it was unrealistic to imagine she might someday sit in a nice little house and read to her grandchildren from them – she took to giving then away one at a time whenever the opportunity arose and she was able to get her hands on new supplies of pens and paper, or even a little book. She usually gave her memoirs to girls and young women, and only if they could read the language – which was always a gamble after generations of geographical and linguistic intermingling.

With his eyes and ears everywhere, Forg developed the role of protector to the little group, adopting as time went on more and more of those traits that had defined Sydell – but without the aloofness.

Cordh continued to search in vain for a suitable partner and at times even toyed with the idea of leaving the group. They were well aware that he would do it without hesitation for the right person.

As for Beauford, he was constantly on the lookout for exquisite delicacies and other rarities from the time before *Day Zero*, sometimes for his own pleasure but often to bring joy to others as well; or he would point something out to them, tell them an interesting story about it and share his knowledge.

No one worried about how long the group would last. It would have been futile – everyone knew that. They preferred to live from day to day, hoping not to fall victim to a roadside ambush, to roaming *hunters* and *scouts*, or to a sudden illness. But in the end, even that was ultimately beyond their control ...

It was a pleasant afternoon when one day they happened across an enchanting spot in the middle of a huge woodland, where the vegetation was so luscious and green that one could only assume they were on the edge of a tropical forest. They had been following the course of a small river for days, until it flowed into a shallow hollow of crystal-clear water, also fed by another, smaller stream. A single outlet at the other end carried the water calmly away. It was more than a pond, however: though it seemed as if the water was not moving at all, a leaf drifting slowly and gently on the surface revealed that its journey was far from over.

A few ruins rose from the shallow depths, their white-washed walls in places surprisingly well-preserved. Here and there a tree broke the surface of the water, while others clung onto the ruins, competing for space with grasses, bushes, mosses, ferns and climbers. The riverbed was almost completely covered with aquatic plants, barely moving in the imperceptible current, like grass encased in crystal clear ice.

Lucia set down her backpack on the riverbank and, with her journal in one hand, walked carefully through the pleasantly cool water that gently caressed the fingers of her other hand. She did not take off her boots, because she did not know what might be hiding in the plants, but if she had not had the journal with her, she would surely have been tempted to swim among the ruins. Regardless, she accepted the refreshing coolness as a gift; all the more so, given the sweltering heat of the forest. It was impossible for someone to sneak up unnoticed here, so she was unafraid to move a few metres further away from the others.

Above the trees – some of them true giants – stretched a flawless blue sky, and the blazing sun cast an enchanting play of light and shadow onto everything. A light breeze rustled the treetops, adding to the beauty of the scene. For the four travellers, this tranquil place was an antidote to the toxic concrete landscape they had left far behind them in terms of space and time, but whose desolation still haunted their minds.

Beauford sat on the moss-covered trunk of a fallen tree, smoked a cigarette and contemplated the butterflies fluttering from blossom to blossom – scattered along the banks was a variety of colourful flowers that nature seemed to have painted *just so* onto the canvas of ubiquitous green; elsewhere, small islands rose from the water, from which flowers stretched their blossoms towards the sun wherever they could find a gap between the treetops high above them.

Cordh and Forg had also taken off their backpacks and laid them against the tree trunk beside those of Lucia and Beauford, while they looked around for firewood and food. The group had unanimously decided to set up camp here until the next morning.

Lucia headed towards the remains of a house.

Stone steps led out of the water and up to the doorless threshold. Through the opening, Lucia could see that the other walls were missing, like the stage wings of a theatre. The floor of the house was covered with moss, and blue and purple blossoms grew here and there. To the left, a tree appeared to lend its crown as a roof to the derelict abode, while to the right, huge ferns had taken up residence and spread themselves across a good half of the room.

Lucia stepped out of the water, took off her boots and socks, and stepped onto the soft carpet of moss that tickled lightly between her toes. She walked to the other side of the open space and looked around. In front of her, she could make out a few fish in the water below, hiding among the plants. Before her were several more ruins in various stages of decay among the plant-covered mounds, while the restless play of dancing light reflected off the water to throw a dappled pattern onto every surface. In the distance, too far off for Lucia to estimate, the edge of the hollow got lost among trees, ferns and flowers whose colours were so intense that they stood out far and wide.

She put down her boots, spread out her socks next to them, and settled down in the lotus position to write down some of her thoughts and impressions of the day.

As the sun dipped further towards the horizon, the shadows became elongated across the hollow and the dancing rays slowly faded, taking with them the muggy heat of the afternoon.

Forg and Cordh returned with a bundle of firewood, a potful of berries and an impressive helping of fish which they had speared with long, thin, sharpened branches. Beauford lit a small campfire, threaded the gutted fish onto sticks, and arranged them around the fire so that each fish would cook slowly and evenly.

"I'll go and look for Lucia," said Cordh, rising.

Beauford and Forg silently watched him as they listened to the soft crackling of the fire and the sounds of the forest, while perceiving the mouth-watering smell of the roasting fish.

"Lucia?" Cordh called again and again as he waded into the shallows and searched around the ruins.

"I'm here!" she answered loudly as he passed in front of the ruin and was about to turn the corner.

"There's fish and sweet berries for dessert," Cordh said, "and Beauford has a cigar for each of us. I don't know when or how he got them." He glanced around him, wondering if there were any water snakes lurking below the surface. It was a silly thought, and he shook his head; after all, it was too late to worry about that now he was thigh-deep.

"Sounds great!" Lucia exclaimed. "I'm on my way!"

The cigars! In all the confusion after they had found Xenos she had forgotten all about them. Beauford must have stashed them away in his backpack and put them to the back of his mind. This final gift from the *Golden City* brought a smile to Lucia's lips.

She finished the sentence she was writing, tore her gaze from the paper, and slammed the journal shut. She looked around her and wondered how quickly the day had passed; she had truly immersed herself in her writing, almost as if she had absorbed everything until it became invisible, only to reappear in a different form.

She stood up, suddenly aware of the effects of sitting for hours in the same position.

Cordh saw Lucia's head through the doorway as she got to her feet.

She stretched her arms and shook her legs which were beginning to tingle. Then she slipped into her socks and damp boots. She picked up the journal and the pencil.

As she turned to make her way towards Cordh, who she could see waiting for her in the water, she noticed words etched in charcoal onto the wall on the right of the doorway. She was surprised she hadn't noticed them sooner because they stood out quite clearly from the whitewash.

She paused and read the lines several times:

We among a few
Bleed upon our nest of dreams
Striving without a banner
Towards the New Sun that shines and waits

Who could have written it, and why here? How long ago? Sydell's tale suddenly came to mind and Lucia speculated that the writer must have something to do with the *Iron Dragonfly*.

She dropped her gaze from the words and walked slowly towards the steps. Only now did she notice that her trousers were virtually dry.

"Everything okay?" asked Cordh, puzzled at Lucia's apparent hesitation to leave the place.

She looked at him and smiled. "Everything's fine."

With that, she ran down the steps into the fresh water to join Cordh and go back to Beauford and Forg, who were waiting for them on the dry bank to share a hearty supper ...

What Lucia had missed, however, and what none of them would ever read, were the words inscribed on the other side of the doorway, concealed behind the large leaves of the ferns growing there:

We among a few
Rise towards our fate
Like a tree in the winds of spring
Holding the banner called hate

The end

?